W9-AFN-809

PATCH

C. H. FRICK

PATCH

HARCOURT, BRACE & WORLD, INC. | New York

The version of the song "I Wonder When I Shall Be Married," which appears on pages 29 and 30, is taken from *Songs of All Time* and is used here with the kind permission of the publishers, Cooperative Recreation Service, Inc., Delaware, Ohio.

PATCH

PATCH

Chapter 1

The loud-speaker squawked once, vibrated, and uttered a tinny announcement. "First call for the mile run! Milers assemble at the south goal post."

Dirk Ingersoll, the student manager, studied the neat score sheet on his clipboard with a pleasant feeling of importance. He ran a finger down a column of figures and turned to a grizzled bear of a man who stood at his elbow.

"So far, Coach, the juniors and seniors are tied."

Coach Anderson grunted absently, his eyes focused on the far end of the field, where the milers were trotting up.

Dirk followed his glance. "There's Grover Godwin. He ought to win this."

Coach Anderson, strolling away, said nothing. Dirk was rechecking the score sheet when a hand touched his elbow. He turned to see a slight, sandy-haired boy.

"Can anyone enter this race?"

"Anyone that wants to run a mile." Dirk looked him over. "Where's your track suit?"

"Track suit? You mean—can't I run like this?"

Dirk shrugged. "Mr. Anderson!" he called, and the coach turned around. "Fellow here wants to know can he race in jeans?"

"No law against it," the coach said, coming over. "But why didn't you dress?"

"Dress? Golly, I thought I did. I thought this was just another assembly—you know, speeches—till everybody headed out here into the stadium."

"Just another assembly?" the coach roared like a wounded lion. "After all the publicity we gave it last month? Announcements in gym classes, articles in the school paper, posters in the halls. . . ." He shook his head. "Two weeks ago I called an organizational meeting and explained the setup. All boys interested in track signed up for their events at that meeting. This assembly is the interclass track meet and varsity tryouts combined. These fellows have been practicing for two weeks. Where were you?"

"Millville."

Mr. Anderson looked a bit dazed. "How did Millville get into this?"

"You asked about it, sir. That's where I was. We moved here three days ago."

"Oh!"

The boy glanced toward the south goal post, where seven or eight boys were jogging about, warming up for the mile. "If I'm supposed to look like the others, I could run in my shorts—maybe?"

The loud-speaker squawked again. "Last call for the mile run!"

The coach grinned. "Keep your pants on and get mov-

4

ing. Report to Tom Martin. He's the letterman in charge of this race. Tell him *I* said it's all right."

"Gee, thanks, but—"

"But what now?"

"But I don't know your name."

The coach chortled. "Anderson."

"*Coach* Anderson," Dirk put in.

"Yes, sir!" The boy was off, charging across the field.

Coach Anderson smiled after him. "He won't run a four-minute mile in those two-ton army boots."

"Here they come up to the starting line," Dirk said a moment later. "He made it."

When Tom Martin had lined up the milers across the track in front of the grandstand, Mr. Anderson moved to the starting line. "Four times around the track," he reminded them for the benefit of the stranger in jeans. "Now on your marks."

The milers hunched forward nervously.

"Get set."

The gun cracked. Eight runners leaped ahead with a spatter of cinders. The ninth, in jeans, jerked up his head, looked startled, and catapulted away.

In the lead was Grover Godwin, already moving smoothly along the pole. A pack of white-suited figures followed, bare legs pumping as they jockeyed for position. The boy in jeans moved up, pounding hard, and passed the pack on the outside. When they headed into the first curve, he lay off Grover's right shoulder.

The crowd watched in near-silence: too early to cheer.

Moving easily, the runners rounded the U-curve at the south end of the track. On the backstretch the pack began to pull slowly apart. The slight figure in jeans was floating along in the lead, followed a few yards back by Grover and then by the others in a lengthening chain.

They rounded the opposite curve and were on the straightaway passing the grandstand. The boy in jeans was romping along a good twenty yards in the lead.

"That kid can *really* run!" Dirk said.

"Poor devil doesn't know how long a mile can be," Mr. Anderson muttered, but Dirk detected a note of hope. "Grover is pacing himself pretty well," the coach continued. "He's not trying to keep up with the kid."

The runners passed the stands at the end of the first lap and moved away.

"Hey!" somebody shouted, pointing. "Look at the patch!"

Dirk saw it too—a glaring blue patch on the right hip of the faded jeans.

"Look at the patch," another shouted.

"Hooray for Patch!"

"Keep going, Patch!"

The runners glided around the south curve and nosed again into the backstretch. The boy in jeans still headed the ever-lengthening chain. But Dirk, watching closely, saw that his strides were shorter now, and the gap between him and Grover was narrowing inch by inch. Grover's knees rose and fell with machine-like precision in the seemingly effortless gait of the picture athlete.

As they entered the straight stretch in front of the stands, the gap was a scant four yards. Grover was closing in without altering his pace.

"Come on, Patch!"

"Get movin', Patch!"

The student body rose and shouted.

At the fifty-yard line Grover put on a burst of speed. The boy in jeans must have heard him coming, for he glanced back over his right shoulder. His head followed Grover's progress as the tall blond swept past him into the lead. Suddenly the boy in jeans slowed and, as Dirk watched appalled, stepped off the track and dropped to one knee on the infield grass.

A groan went up from the crowd. "Gah," Coach Anderson snorted. "Front runner. Only two laps. And how I could have used a good miler!"

Dirk trotted along the edge of the track and leaned over the boy as he knelt on the grass. "What happened? You had a lot left."

"Still have." The boy was fumbling with a shoelace. "Anchors," he panted. He jerked off one heavy boot, flung it aside, and started yanking at the lace of the second boot. Dirk was watching the other runners glide past when he heard the boy talking.

"Who's this Patch everybody's yelling for?"

Dirk looked down and grinned. "*You!*"

A look of amazement spread across the boy's face, followed by one of sheer joy. He stared at Dirk a second, tore off the other boot, and leaped back onto the track in his socks.

Dirk winced. The last trailing runner had just passed, and Patch took out after him, his stockinged feet pounding the sharp cinders. He passed the last man and drew abreast of the man just ahead. Dirk saw Patch flinch and break stride. He hobbled a few yards farther, glanced

7

back, limped diagonally across the track to the outside, and stepped off onto the grass.

This time Dirk groaned.

"On-again, off-again," somebody shouted.

"One down!" came a gleeful cry.

But Patch was off and running on the narrow rim of grass along the outer edge of the track. Now he was last again, and Grover was far ahead, already on the backstretch.

Around the south end of the oval swept the other runners, Patch on the outside like a shadow. Dirk watched him across the field as the milers moved along onto the backstretch. Patch was running easily now with a smooth, rhythmical stride that contrasted sharply with the disjointed movements of the tiring tailenders. Two stragglers were running in jerky slow-motion, like an old phonograph running down. But Patch was already well beyond them, pulling abreast of the middle group. As he entered the north curve, Grover was coming off it onto the straightaway, running smoothly, tirelessly, as if he could hold the pace forever.

Grover passed the starting line and began the last lap with a lead that looked insurmountable.

"Love to watch that guy run," said Dirk.

"Gah," said Anderson.

"What's wrong?"

"Those knees that are flashing so high and so pretty. If he'd keep them a little lower, he wouldn't run out of steam toward the end. Those long, reaching strides. If he'd keep them a few inches shorter, he'd have more push—and less pulling to do."

8

Dirk sighed. "Looks beautiful to me."

"That's the trouble. Everyone tells him so, and what's the coach's opinion against the school's?"

"Well," Dirk said slowly, "he *did* win first in the city last year in the mile."

"Last year's crop of milers was mediocre. Actually, Grover's best distance is the half-mile, even though he didn't win it. . . . Look, he's tiring."

Dirk studied the runners as they struggled along the backstretch in the final lap. "Yeah. That little sophomore —fellow who ran all week with a stop watch in his hand —he's moving up."

"It's just that Grover's coming back to him. That's Benny Chapnik. He's made up ten yards, but he still has forty left to make up." The coach shook his head.

"He doesn't look like a runner to me," Dirk said. "Kind of shuffles along."

"Nice economy of form, that Chapnik. Too tense though."

As they watched, Patch in his outside "lane" moved closer to Benny Chapnik and swept on past him. The runners were rounding the last curve.

"I wonder how many extra yards that fellow's run, taking the outside," mused Dirk.

"This track isn't wide, and he had the pole for two laps. Still, if you run a mile in the second lane, they say you go eighteen yards farther than the man on the in-side—"

"Hey, look at the kid cut loose!"

Unleashing a sudden burst of speed as he hit the head of the homestretch, the boy in jeans came driving for the tape. The gap that had been shrinking by inches began to close a foot at a stride. The fans were shouting his name as Patch came roaring toward them along the grassy edge of the track.

Grover, hearing the tumult, glanced behind him. He saw Benny Chapnik inching closer on the crunching cinders. But Benny was still a safe twenty yards behind. Grover did not seem to notice Patch, gliding silently along on the grass.

Coach Anderson smelled trouble. He jerked into action. "Move the tape!" he shouted. "Move over. Move the tape!" But the two students who were holding the tape across the track stood at the finish line as immobile as posts. Anderson shouted louder. "Move! Get over onto the grass!" But again his words were drowned by the din.

Patch, on the grass, zipped past to the right of the tape. It was still taut and untouched a split second later when Grover Godwin snapped it with his chest. It fluttered to the track.

The student nearest to Coach Anderson stood holding one end of the broken string. He looked from Patch to Grover to the tape and then turned blankly to the coach. "Who won?"

As if in answer to the question, a spontaneous cheer rose for Patch. His name filled the air.

Dirk glued his eyes to the score sheet and jotted down the results as Coach Anderson called them off. "Chapnik, third . . . Warner, fourth . . . Bauer, fifth," the coach snapped as the runners crossed the line.

". . . and Tompkins sixth. That's all. The others dropped out."

A hand grabbed Dirk's arm. Grover Godwin, rasping for breath, asked hoarsely, "Got me—for first?"

"Second," Dirk said.

"I—" Grover protested, gulping in air, "broke the tape."

Coach Anderson turned to Dirk. "Do you know the name of the kid who won?"

Dirk shook his head.

"Bring him over here."

The boy was nearby, panting and grinning as the other runners gathered about, puffing congratulations.

"Hey, Patch," Dirk called.

"My name's—not really Patch," he panted. "It's Sherrill."

"From now on," said Dirk, "I'll bet it's Patch."

"But why?"

Dirk pointed to the bright-blue rectangle on the jeans. Patch twisted around. "Oh, that? Naw. My little brother got the patch. This is where it came from."

One of the boys leaned over to verify. "That's right. No patch. The pocket's gone."

"Well, now that that's settled," said Dirk, "the coach wants to see you."

Grover's voice reached them even before they joined the group. "He sneaked past me out on the grass. I couldn't hear him coming or I could've speeded up."

"The guy didn't run on the track," protested Sax Warner, who finished fourth. "I thought you had to run on the track."

"Well, he sure didn't cut any corners," Coach Anderson rumbled. "He took the long way around." He caught a glimpse of Patch and thrust out a huge hand. "Congratulations. You ran a good race, though somewhat—uh —individualistic. What's your name?"

"Finnegan," Sax Warner answered for him with a sniff. "Off-Again-On-Again-Finnegan."

"Jones," said Patch.

"I still say," insisted Grover, "that I broke the tape. If that doesn't make me the winner, why have a tape?"

Patch looked at him curiously, then glanced around at the circle of tense white faces. His own was frankly puzzled. "What does it matter?"

"Huh?"

"Who cares who won?" Patch asked. "I sure don't. I was just running for fun—and I had it." His eyes crinkled with laughter.

A circle of stares looked back at him.

"Well, I guess I better put my shoes on," Patch murmured. He turned and walked away in his stocking feet.

Chapter 2

Dirk was sorting jerseys the next afternoon when he heard Grover and Sax come clattering into the locker room. Grover, tall and blondly elegant in a chartreuse flannel shirt, was followed by the stocky, swarthy Sax in a black turtle-neck sweater. They brushed past Dirk and hurried straight to the bulletin board, where the names of the track squad members were posted.

Dirk waited. Presently he heard Grover's footsteps coming toward him. "Tell Anderson I want to talk to him."

Dirk looked up mildly from his work. "Mr. Anderson is already out on the field." He was half tempted to bow and add, "Sir."

"He's made a mistake," Grover said. "These three men he listed as milers—myself, Jones, and Chapnik—"

Dirk nodded. "But listed in slightly different order."

Grover flushed. "That Jones, that boy they call Patch, he withdrew from the race."

"Oh?" Dirk asked. "When?"

"After it was over. You were there. You heard him."

13

"Matter of fact, I didn't. I only heard him say he didn't care who won."

"Well, I care," blurted Sax Warner. "He ran an illegal race. He should have been disqualified."

"Sure," agreed Grover. "That would leave me, Chapnik, and Sax as the three milers. Sax was a miler on last year's squad. He deserves consideration for that."

"More than consideration," grumbled Sax. "I deserve a letter-sweater."

"If you'd earned enough points in meets last year," Dirk pointed out, "you'd have one."

"That's just it! If I couldn't get one last year when I was running the mile and the half-mile, what are my chances this year running only the half? I'm not out for track for my health. Either I run in both events—or neither."

Dirk shrugged. "You know how the system works, Sax. Like the Olympic tryouts. Anyone who finishes first, second, or third in the tryouts makes the squad— in that event. In the half-mile you finished second; in the mile you finished fourth. So you run the 880 only. Sure, ask the coach. But that's what he'll tell you."

"Then you can keep the track clothes," Sax said. "I'll sit this season out."

"Now wait a minute, Sax." Grover put a restraining hand on his arm. "That new kid," he said to Dirk, "isn't eligible. He just moved to town."

"That's been checked," Dirk answered. "He'll be eligible before the first meet." He turned to Sax. "Do you want your gear or don't you?"

14

Sax glowered.

"He wants it," Grover said.

Both boys had dressed and gone out to the track when Patch came in.

"You said I should come here after school?"

I should have said *right* after school, Dirk thought. He said, "I didn't have time just then to explain. Look at the list on the bulletin board."

Patch read the typed announcement:

The following men will comprise the West High School track team. All men whose names appear on this list will report for practice after school every afternoon until further notice. Equipment to be checked out from Dirk Ingersoll, student manager, today.

JOHN ANDERSON, Coach

"I thought I was just running a race!" Patch turned to Dirk with a grin. "Life was simple in Millville, but here I never know what I'll be getting into next."

"Nobody," Dirk said stiffly, "*has* to be on the track team. Nobody gets begged."

"Golly, it sounds wonderful. I love to run. But Millville didn't even have a track team. And I don't know how I made this one."

"You tried out for it."

"I did?"

"That assembly yesterday—that was the interclass track meet and varsity tryouts combined. Mr. Anderson

15

told you yesterday, but I guess you didn't take it in. It's a neat little scheme the coach worked out to open the track season with a bang. There's a trophy for the winning class, so the classes see to it that their best men come out. The top three finishers in each event make up the varsity squad." Dirk was looking at Patch's feet as he talked. "What size?"

"Eight and a half."

"Better try these on."

"Real track shoes!" Patch said, reaching out eagerly. He turned them over. "With spikes—six of them."

"Try them on with your feet bare. The shoes will stretch some with use."

Patch worked one on. "It feels like a glove," he said proudly, "soft and snug."

"Good. Can you move your toes? . . . Okay, now jersey, pants, sweat suit. . . . Hurry and get into these things while I look up your locker number and combination. We're both overdue on the field. Everyone else is out there already, and Mr. Anderson probably wants to make a speech."

Dirk felt clairvoyant when the coach tootled his whistle just as they appeared on the field.

"Come over here in the stands, all of you," he roared. "I want to make a few things crystal-clear."

They huddled together in their sweat suits, the chill wind of early March whistling around their ears, their arms crossed and their hands pushed into their armpits for warmth.

"This will take about three minutes," the coach began.

16

"The rest of the time for the next ten weeks you'll be out there working and sweating. *Work* is the keynote. Work —and enjoy it! From the beginning of time men have been running and jumping and throwing things—just for fun. You'll learn to relax, mentally and physically— to work relaxed, to run relaxed, even in the dashes. You'll learn that no sport can touch this for sheer enjoyment. But you'll rob yourself of pleasure if you give it less than your best.

"You think that because you made the track team you're pretty good. I hope you're right. But your competition was softer than any you'll ever face again. From now on things will get tougher. Tougher with every meet. And our first meet is less than a month away."

Dirk looked around. The sophomore with the thin, dark face, Benny Chapnik, was leaning forward as if reaching for every word. Sophisticated seniors Grover and Sax, behind the broad back of Moose Elliot, were already playing ticktacktoe in the dust of the bleacher seat between them. Mr. Anderson seemed to sense it, almost as if he could see through Moose, of all people. His next words were:

"You who were on the squad last year. The records you made—the speed you ran, the height you jumped— should be like last year's clothes: outgrown!

"You who are new this year," he went on, "look around you. There are twenty-eight men on this squad, competing in thirteen events, including the relays. That means I can't spend very much time with any one man, and that's good. The thing a man learns for himself he learns best, and he learns initiative with it. When you

17

need me, I'm here. I'm here to tell you how to get started and where you seem to be going astray. But you're not going to be identical disks stamped from a single mold. Most of the great athletes developed their own styles: Charley Paddock in the sprints, Paavo Nurmi in the distances, Parry O'Brien in the shot-put. Copy them if you want to, but remember that your body is uniquely your own, like your mind, and try to find the technique that works best for you. Then I'll come along with suggestions."

Dirk wondered if the styles of those all-time greats—or even their names—were known to some of these boys. He glanced at Patch sitting beside him, but Patch seemed to be in a world of his own. He was staring out on the field, entranced by the wooden hurdles, the shot, the height of the pole-vault standards. He acted, Dirk thought, as if he were seeing such things for the first time. And perhaps he was.

"Somebody asked about training rules," the coach continued. "Well, we just try to use horse sense. Eat as you've always eaten—regular, balanced meals—except on the day of a meet, and I'll talk about that when the time comes. Try to avoid foods that are hard to digest—rich spices and foods fried in grease. If the pie crust is soggy, do as someone suggested: 'Eat the inside and admire the crust.' If you want candy and sweets—and my guess is you do—eat them right after meals, *in moderation*. Don't eat between meals. The whole idea is simply to feel your best. You'll feel better if you get nine hours' sleep; you'll need it. You'll do better if you don't smoke —so don't!

"Before every practice, remember, *always* warm up. Loosen those muscles. We want no shin splints or pulled muscles that we can prevent.

"Now go out and show me the warm-ups I showed you last week. Then work like demons, because that's how track stars are made."

With a whoop the twenty-eight boys leaped to the field. Patch leaped too and then stood looking around at the bewildering flurry of arms and legs. Some of the boys were standing on their shoulders and pedaling air with their legs. Others kept bending over and swinging their arms to touch alternate toes. Still others were doing push-ups, while a few were running in place and lifting their knees higher and higher.

A hand zipped past under Patch's chin, and he jumped back.

"No statues here, please." It was Sax Warner, swinging his arms wide and suspiciously close as he rotated his trunk from side to side.

Patch saw a boy on the ground who seemed to be doing a split and was bending forward and touching his right foot with both hands. Patch tried it too.

"That's for hurdlers, you dope," Sax called in a voice unnecessarily loud.

Patch scrambled to his feet and started jogging in place, lifting his knees higher and higher until he heard the whistle again.

"Milers and 880 men come over here," Coach Anderson called.

When five boys had gathered around him, the coach said, "Three of you are new to the squad this year, and

19

I want to explain a few things. We train for the mile and half-mile by under-and-over-the-distance running. That means you milers won't do many mile runs in practice. Once in a while you'll run *two* miles without stopping. Or do a 660. Or try a 220 at sprint speed. But most of the time you'll be running quarters. That's to learn pace." He stopped. "Know what pace means?" he asked Benny Chapnik.

Benny raised his large dark eyes and nodded soberly.

"Sure," Sax whispered. "He runs with a clock in his hand."

Benny said nothing, but his fingers tightened over his stop watch.

"You know what pace is?" the coach asked Patch.

Patch shook his head.

"Obviously not," Sax remarked. "Judging from yesterday's race, he thinks he's part hare and part tortoise."

"*You* were the one, Sax," the coach snapped, "who ran like a tortoise." Even Grover guffawed. "All of you," Anderson continued, "are going to learn pace. First for a five-minute mile. Later we'll speed it up. Start today with a seventy-five-second quarter, Grover setting the pace. Then walk for a couple of minutes and run another seventy-five-second quarter. Walk after every run. Keep doing seventy-five-second quarters until I tell you to stop."

He walked away to talk to another group.

"Well, my little ones," Grover said, "let's get moving. I'll set the pace. Try to stick with me."

Benny Chapnik held out his stop watch. "Would you like to borrow this?"

Grover waved it aside. "An experienced runner doesn't bother to carry a stop watch. He can judge lap time within a second."

Benny drew back his hand. "Paavo Nurmi," he murmured, "always carried a stop watch."

Sax snickered. "Paavo Godwin doesn't need one." He turned to Benny. "Nurmi your hero, kid? Kind of outdated, isn't he?"

"His style isn't." Benny spoke with the slightest hint of an accent. "One learns from many people."

"One does, does one? You're a foreigner, aren't you? One of those refugees?"

"I'm an American now."

"Cut the chitchat, you guys," Grover said. "Anderson's watching. Here we go."

Dirk was still lugging equipment inside when the last spattering shower was turned off, leaving the shower room in sudden silence. A voice rose.

"The zigzag kid from Millville acts like a wild horse spending his first afternoon in harness. He's just found out that the mile consists mostly of pace running."

Dirk saw Patch raise his head and stop with one leg in his jeans.

"Do a lap in seventy-five," the voice continued. "Do another. . . . And another. . . . He'll find out. Work like demons? Nah. Work like plow horses. Work like slaves."

Dirk watched Patch yank up his jeans, slip into moccasins, and reach for his jacket. He pulled it on quickly, headed for the door, and was gone. Slowly the door swung to. Just before it closed, Dirk could have sworn he heard a faint chuckle come drifting back.

"'One rose doth not a summer make,'" the strident voice went on. "Guy that wrote that should have added, 'One win doth not a runner make.'"

"Sax," Dirk called. "You can knock it off. Your boy's gone."

Sax came storming out in his shorts and socks. "What do you mean, Ingersoll?"

"I mean he's too far away to hear."

"Funny man."

"And what's more, I think your campaign is doomed to failure."

"What campaign? You know all about it, I guess?"

"Well, it isn't too subtle to figure. You're trying to talk him or heckle him off the squad. But it won't work."

"Why won't it work?"

"Look at his face when he's running. That kid loves to run. Maybe it's drudgery to you, but you'll never convince Patch."

Sax smiled knowingly. "You're no psychologist, Dirk. You heard him after yesterday's race. 'Who cares who won?' he asks—like it's funny. Who cares! A fellow who doesn't care if he wins won't care to slave for hours and weeks of practice. You practice so you'll improve. Well, anyhow, that's the idea. Some of us practice because we have to, to stay on the team. But this guy—he doesn't even care if he wins. So why improve? So why practice?" He spread his hands.

"Well—" Dirk rubbed his palm back and forth over his stubbly hair. "I still think you're wrong, Sax. This character doesn't follow a pattern. Maybe he doesn't even make sense. But he loves to run, so he'll stick. You're working on the wrong man."

"You mean"—Sax looked at him searchingly and lowered his voice—"the foreigner?"

Dirk snorted. "Leave 'em both alone. All you want is a letter-sweater. Then why not earn it—in the half-mile? Keep training rules, leave your car in the garage, run more—"

"Fine, fatherly advice, Dirk," Grover said as he came out buttoning his chartreuse shirt. "But how can he finish better than second? I'm still the number one half-miler at West, as you saw again yesterday. Whenever Sax runs the 880, I'll be there too."

"Let him pick up enough seconds then. Not that I think you're invincible, Grover."

Grover shrugged and strolled back to his locker. Sax studied him a moment with narrowed eyes and then followed thoughtfully after.

Chapter 3

Fifteen minutes later Dirk was homeward bound, wheeling his rattly sedan around a curve in the old River Road as the shadows lengthened. He nosed out of the curve and saw a boy jogging along the road ahead. The setting sun glinted on sandy hair, and Dirk pulled to a stop.

"Want a ride, Patch?" he called.

Patch jogged over to the car. "You live out this way?" he asked in surprise.

"About a mile down the road," Dirk said. "Where do you live?"

"Couple of miles beyond that."

"Climb in. I'll take you home."

Patch shook his head. "I'll ride with you as far as you go though," he said as he opened the door.

"You've already come three miles," Dirk said, easing the car into high. "I'll take you the rest of the way. Why, you must live six miles from school. Of course, you missed the school bus by staying for practice—"

Patch laughed. "That makes it seem more like home.

I was always missing the school bus in Millville. Our farm was five miles out."

"So you had to walk?"

"Oh, I ran. Walking's too slow."

"Do you run *every*where?"

"Just about."

Dirk shook his head. "Me, I couldn't run four laps around a bass drum."

Patch laughed again. "Well, you own a car." He started to whistle a tune, gay and plaintive as a mountain ballad. After a moment he broke off. "Maybe I never grew up," he said. "You know how kids love to run? I just never got over it. I'd still run for the train if I could."

"Run for the train?"

"Where we lived near Millville, a train came through every afternoon. I'd hear its whistle and take off—over our hill and down, and up another and down. While I was taking the short cut, the train was curving around the hills, going the long way. I'd get there in time to wave, and then I'd have to hurry back before Dad missed me from the field."

"Whew. How far?"

"From the field to the tracks was—oh, maybe a mile. Of course, when I was a little kid I never quite made it in time, but I kept trying. I'd stand on the second hill and watch the train go by. Finally I got all the way. And then the trainmen got so they knew me and waved." He was quiet a moment. "I wonder if they know we've moved away."

"How did you happen to move?"

25

"Dad's always hankered for bottom land. More and more as we got less rain in the summers. Till one day he said he'd found a farm in the bottoms near Crescent City —cheap. So here we are. He's always that way—kind of notionate." Patch picked up the tune where he had left off and whistled softly.

A moment later he broke off again. "Right around the next curve," he said.

They rounded a clump of willows, and Dirk saw a frame house built on stilts.

"Funny-looking, isn't it?" Patch said. "Mom says it looks like a big bird. Dad says just so it isn't a stork."

Dirk pulled off the road and stopped at the battered gate. "You can ride out with me every night after practice."

"Thanks, I'd like that—but only as far as you go. You shouldn't have to go out of your way again. And besides, I'll need to stretch my legs a little." Patch leaped out and slammed the door.

Dirk tilted his head and listened. "What's the music?"

"Oh, that? C'mon in and see."

Dirk was torn between curiosity and the urge to get home to dinner. He slid out from under the wheel. "I can't stay but a minute."

Patch loped ahead down the path that led to the house on stilts. He turned, waved Dirk along, and disappeared momentarily among the long shadows near the house and the tall bushes veiled in early-spring green. He reappeared on the steep wooden stairs and waited outside the door.

Dirk walked down the rutted path and heard voices rising in song. He could catch the words now. First a woman's voice, high and sweet and smooth as honey, singing,

I'm a-goin' down this road feelin' bad . . .

Then a deep voice and many childlike ones chiming in,

I'm a-goin' down this road feelin' bad . . .

Every gay voice, Dirk noted, belied the words of the song. He trudged up the rickety open stairs, and the two boys started to enter the house together.

I'm a-goin' down where the climate suits my clothes,

the sweet voice sang.

The door creaked raucously as Patch pushed it open.

"That you, Shirl?" the voice called.

Dirk wondered vaguely who Shirl could be till he remembered that Patch's first name was Sherrill.

"Yes'm," Patch said as they stepped inside, into a large, uncarpeted room. An iron monster of a stove dominated the room. Near it on the floor sat a cluster of children at the feet of a slim red-haired woman. On the fringe, sprawled in an easy chair, was a man in overalls, his eyes the same amazing blue as Patch's.

"Mother and Father," Patch mumbled, as if unaccustomed to the words, "this is Dirk Ingersoll."

"Come join us," Mr. Jones rumbled, waving a casual hand. "These here are Joneses too," he added, indicating the children. "That's what's meant by keeping up with the Joneses."

27

"We sing 'most every night afta suppah," Mrs. Jones said with a pleasant smile. Her southern accent surprised Dirk, for Patch's was just plain Hoosier. "Where you been, Shirl?" she asked, turning to him. "We ate early tonight. Your daddy was hungry."

"I been practicing track. I'm on the track team," Patch said proudly.

"Track team?" She sounded vague. "Well, that's real nice. I kep' your suppah warm for you, Shirl."

"I'd better go," Dirk said. "Uh—I'm late too."

"Oh, can't you sing with us a little?" she asked. "You know any ballads or mountain songs? 'Springfield Mountain'? 'Barbara Allen'? 'Lord Randal, My Son'? 'Foggy, Foggy Dew'?"

Dirk shook his head.

"Oh, pshaw." She was strumming her fingers across a long, slender stringed instrument that lay on her lap.

"I'd like it, Mrs. Jones, if you'd play something on that —uh—"

"Dulcimer," she said. "My daddy down in Tennessee made it for me before I left the mountains—when I was married." She spoke wistfully, as if it were more than a matter of miles from the Ohio River bottoms to the Smoky Mountains. She started to sing very softly.

> *Down in the valley, valley so low,*
> *Hang your head over, hear the wind blow.*

She broke off, and Dirk said, "It's beautiful. Walnut, isn't it? And that white wood along the edges?"

"Holly." She drew her fingers gently across the strings,

and the box gave forth dulcet tones. She sang again very softly.

Now the holly bears a berry as white as the milk,
And Mary bore Jesus, who was wrapped up in silk.

"Oh, Shirl," Mr. Jones put in. "Aunt Rhody had her kittens."

"Good! How many?"

"Five. In the bureau drawer."

"Whose drawer?"

"Mine," Mr. Jones said, looking honored. He pointed across the room. Against the far wall stood a chest of drawers, one drawer hanging open. Dirk listened closely and could detect faint mewing sounds.

And the first tree of the greenwood, it was holly,

Mrs. Jones sang, and the song was ended.

"Let's sing 'I Wonder When I Shall Be Married,'" Mr. Jones suggested. The small Joneses clapped and shrieked with joy, and from the midst of the circle came violent piglike squeaks. Everyone else ignored them, and Dirk tried hard to do likewise. The Joneses raised their voices in song, and the squeals died away.

I wonder when I shall be married, Oh, be married, Oh,
*   be married,*
I wonder when I shall be married, for my beauty's begin-
*   ning to fade.*
My mother she is so willing, Oh, so willing, Oh, so will-
*   ing*
My mother she is so willing, for she's four daughters
*   besides. . . .*

29

Dirk looked around at all the Joneses singing lustily and found himself joining in.

My shoes have gone to be mended, Oh, be mended, Oh,
*   be mended,*
And my petticoat to be dyed green.
And they will be ready by Sunday, Oh, by Sunday, Oh,
*   by Sunday,*
Oh, say! Won't I look like a queen?
A cup, a spoon, and a trencher, Oh, a trencher, Oh, a
*   trencher,*
And a candle-stick made out of clay.
Oh, say! Won't I be a bargain, Oh, a bargain, Oh, a bar-
*   gain,*
For someone to carry away?
I wonder when I shall be married, Oh, be married, Oh,
*   be married,*
I wonder when I shall be married, for my beauty's begin-
*   ning to fade.*

Dirk applauded vigorously and called, "Encore!"

"How 'bout 'Blue-Tailed Fly'?" Patch asked.

Again the small Joneses clapped and shrieked with joy, and again from the midst of the circle came shrill piglike squeals.

"Raig'n!" Mr. Jones exploded. "I told you to tie that pig to the table leg."

A red-headed eight-year-old glanced up. "But why?"

"Like I told you. You tie a pig by a hind leg or by his tail, and he won't squeal."

"Why won't he?"

"How do I know what a pig thinks? I just know he

30

won't squeal. Farmers learn things like that. Do it, or out he goes where he belongs."

Raig'n rose reluctantly and carried his pet across the room to a table. Dirk noticed the knee of his jeans and wondered if the blue rectangle, obviously not provided by the manufacturer, was the pocket that had given Patch his nickname. As Raig'n struggled manfully with his piglet, the other children sat watching with sorrowful faces.

" 'The Blue-Tailed Fly'?" Dirk asked, smiling. "Then I really do have to go."

Five minutes later he was descending the swaying steps. He started to trudge up the rutted path, singing,

Jimmy crack corn, and I don't care . . .

He slid under the wheel and pressed the starter. . . . I should have warned Patch about Sax, he thought. . . . But somehow, Sax Warner seemed far away. Dirk drove along whistling "The Blue-Tailed Fly."

Chapter 4

Three weeks of varsity practice have made a difference, Dirk thought one afternoon many days later. He watched the boys skimming the hurdles, tossing the shot, and gliding around the cinder oval almost like veterans. He glanced at his watch. Five o'clock and still no announcement.

Across the field Mr. Anderson was working on starts with the dashmen. Dirk headed across the field to remind him and was halfway across when the whistle shrilled.

"Into the bleachers, men, all of you," Coach Anderson shouted.

The boys scrambled over the rail and onto the bleacher seats, eager to hear the long-awaited announcement.

"The State Relays," the coach began when all had assembled, "are Saturday—the day after tomorrow. They're held annually on the last Saturday in March."

All faces were lifted toward his. Nothing he had said yet was news, but at least he was on the right subject.

"This extravaganza is sometimes called the world's largest indoor high school track meet. Last year nine

32

hundred athletes from about sixty high schools in the state competed. This year's meet will probably attract even more."

The boys stirred restlessly and waited.

"Those who enter," the coach continued, "compete as individuals rather than as a team. No school, as far as I know, will send its entire team. Here in Crescent City only three of the high schools are sending men."

"Who's going from West?" someone asked in a loud whisper.

Mr. Anderson ignored it and continued. "This meet is held inside the University Fieldhouse. It's *indoor* track. Some say that's an entirely different sport from outdoor track."

Sax called out, "I see by the morning paper that you're taking fifteen men. Who are they?"

The coach pulled a list from his pocket and unfolded it slowly. "I wish I could take every one of you," he said, "but limits had to be imposed for this meet. You'll all be competing in the regular meets that start next week. I also wish that we could have had a couple more weeks of practice, but every coach in the state wishes that. We all had to wait for the weather to warm up a little."

"Read the list!" somebody muttered.

"I'm taking one man in each event," the coach announced, "plus the sprint relay team and the shuttle-hurdle relay team. These men will make the trip: broad jump, Martin; shot-put, Elliot; half-mile, Godwin; mile, Jones. . . ." He read on as the team sat in tense silence.

"Now get this!" he said, folding the list and shoving it into his pocket. "We'll go by chartered bus, leaving here Saturday morning at 8:30. It's a three-hour drive. Eat a good breakfast at home because you won't be having much lunch—probably only toast with honey and a cup of tea."

Somebody snickered, but the coach continued unhearing.

"You men whose names I read, be at the fieldhouse door at 8:30, kit in hand. Get everything ready before you leave here this afternoon! That means uniforms—Dirk will issue you new ones as soon as we get inside—sweat suits, socks or pushers as you prefer, track shoes. . . . Dirk will issue new laces this afternoon. A broken shoestring can cost you a race. . . .

"There'll be no practice tomorrow. Go to the showers now."

The group broke up and began to move across the field, some racing ahead, others strolling and talking excitedly.

"Don't forget your track shoes, Moose," somebody called. "Nobody could lend you a pair of size 12 D's."

Dirk walked over to congratulate Patch on his selection. Benny was already with him doing the same. Dirk looked around and saw that Grover and Sax were wending their separate ways, silently, thoughtfully, across the field.

"About indoor tracks," Benny was saying eagerly. "I've read about them. They're boards, you know, not cinders. And they're not so large as the standard outdoor tracks. On indoor tracks there are usually eleven laps to the mile—instead of four—which makes a lot of turns in a mile. The turns are banked. They have a steep slope to the inside, and that calls for a special technique. Mal Whitfield figured out how to run them—"

"Mal Whitfield?" Patch asked.

"Whitfield, two-time Olympic 800-meter champ," Benny said quickly and then continued. "He says the way to run on an indoor track is to *accelerate going into* the turns. Will you remember that, Patch? It might help."

Patch nodded uncertainly.

"Well," Dirk put in slowly, not wanting to embarrass Benny, "you're right about indoor tracks in general, especially the so-called big ones like Madison Square Garden. But I went up to the State Relays last year, and the track in the University Fieldhouse is cinder. And flat."

"Oh?" Benny thought a moment. "How large?"

"I'd say 220. I seem to recall eight laps to the mile."

Benny studied the problem. "In that case, Patch," he said finally, "I believe you'll find running conditions similar to those here." His face brightened. "And that's good! I hope you win."

He gripped Patch's hand and left them, running ahead in his shuffling gait.

"Nice fellow," Dirk said.

Patch nodded agreement. "But he worries too much. He ought to just let himself go and enjoy things."

"Dirk!" someone called from the doorway. "Where are those new uniforms?"

Dirk dug in like a dashman and took off toward his job.

He had handed out fourteen new jerseys, fourteen

pants, and fourteen pairs of laces. If only Grover would come and claim his, Dirk could go out and bring in the equipment. He sat on the edge of the table and waited.

In the distance the showers were spattering and the boys were chattering, but gradually Dirk became aware of voices much closer. Behind him the door to the coach's office stood open.

"I've told you the basis," Mr. Anderson's voice rumbled. "Performance."

The next words were almost inaudible; then Anderson's voice came again.

"The reason you haven't run a race since the tryouts is that I'm the coach. I believe that milers should run *within themselves* except in actual meets. I don't want my runners tense. I don't want my runners exhausted. I want them relaxed and ready."

Again Dirk heard a murmur of protest, followed once more by the coach's words.

"No, I don't know what Patch can do, but I intend to find out. He's one of those rare natural runners. My guess is, he can do plenty! Maybe a new city record, maybe more."

Once more Dirk heard the murmuring voice and the coach's angry reply.

"So what? What good is last year's champion if he's out of condition? Your time in the tryouts this spring would never win a blue ribbon in a regular meet. . . . Sure it was early—early March, don't I know? But you should have been working out sooner, instead of just riding around in your new convertible. . . . Forget about being city champ! Last year is over. And just between us, you were lucky. It was an off-year for local milers. Once we'd moved on to bigger things—the Petersburg Relays and the Ohio Valley meet—you were outclassed. It's my guess that this year you'll have to be a lot faster if you hope to repeat even as city champion, and you haven't shown any marked improvement so far. So Patch is my choice, and that's final."

A moment later Grover emerged from the office redfaced and still in his sweat suit. He glanced down at the table. "Mine?" he asked, picking up the small pile of clothing.

Dirk nodded, wishing he'd been two blocks away from the conversation he had inadvertently overheard.

Uniform in hand, Grover hesitated. He looked at Dirk slowly and searchingly—as if, Dirk thought, trying to ascertain without asking how much he had heard. Head high, Grover turned and walked to his locker.

Chapter 5

Even down in the dressing rooms the excitement of a momentous occasion hung over the University Fieldhouse. The dressing rooms teemed with adolescents and vigor, with boys and noise and harried coaches.

"Hurry and get into your track clothes," Coach Anderson said, "so we can get upstairs to some elbow room."

While the athletes were changing, Dirk unpacked the towels, batons, and miscellaneous equipment. He started around the group to distribute towels and came last to Patch.

Patch was on his knees, rummaging frantically in his duffel bag. He looked up when he saw Dirk's feet beside him. "They aren't here!"

"What aren't here?"

"My shoes! My track shoes—"

"Of course they are. Here, let me look." Dirk dropped to his knees, but a moment's inspection showed him that Patch was right. He turned to Patch with an empty feeling. "You forgot to pack them."

Patch looked aghast. "Oh, *no*—"

"Do you remember putting them in your bag?"

"Why, yes—I thought I did."

Coach Anderson's big voice rose above the clamor and yammer of the dressing room. "Everybody upstairs now. Get up there and jog around a bit. Go through your warm-ups. Get those muscles loose. Upstairs now!"

"Go on up with the others," Dirk told Patch. "In your socks. I'll stay down here and look around."

Fifteen minutes later Dirk trudged up the long ramp and emerged in the cavernous fieldhouse. It was swarming with athletes. He searched for the West High contingent and finally spotted the burly, gray-thatched coach just calling his men around him. The meet was about to begin.

As he rejoined the group, Dirk saw Patch looking at him hopefully and shook his head. The loud-speaker boomed out the call for the first race, the sixty-yard dash. Bill Adams was sent on his way, propelled by a flurry of well-placed pats.

"Bill ought to take this heat without any trouble," someone said.

Mr. Anderson frowned. "We don't know a thing about anyone else in this race. We only know that the hundred, not the sixty, is Bill's best distance. So don't expect the moon." He looked around. "Patch, quit prancing around in your socks."

Patch gulped and took a deep breath. "I can't find my shoes," he said in a firm voice.

"What! Oh, now—"

"That's right, Mr. Anderson," Dirk put in. "He thinks he packed them, but they're not in his bag. I checked and they just don't seem to be anywhere."

39

"Any of you fellows know anything about Patch's shoes?" the coach boomed.

A circle of blank faces stared at him silently.

"Well," the coach rumbled, "this beats it." He whirled on Patch. "You *think* you packed them. But do you *know?*"

"I—"

"They're at the starting line," someone called.

The gun cracked, and a wisp of white smoke drifted upward. Chest and chest the runners leaped forward as if jet-propelled. In only a matter of seconds they reached the tape, still almost shoulder to shoulder.

Anderson shook his head in disappointment. "Close though," he murmured.

Bill Adams came trotting up, puffing apologies. "Just didn't seem to have time to get rolling. Sorry, Mr. Anderson."

Anderson nodded and sent Mike Montgomery out in response to the call for the sixty-yard high hurdles. Then he turned back to Bill Adams.

"Jones here seems to be shoeless."

"Not again," Bill said with a chuckle. "What happened?"

The coach shrugged. "From now on, so help me, the manager will take all shoes to the meet, even if he has to carry a pack as big as Santa's. But right now—would you mind if Patch wore your shoes in the mile?"

"No, sure. I won't need them again," he added ruefully, "till the relays, and they come last. Golly, I thought sure I'd qualify in the trials." He shook his head. "Here,

40

Patch, try these on." As he handed them over he looked at Patch's feet. "They're too big for you, I'm afraid."

"Only Benny Chapnik wears Patch's size," Dirk put in, "and he's not here."

Patch slid into the shoes gratefully. "Well, I sure can wiggle my toes," he said, grinning.

"Might as well keep them on so you'll be ready when they call the mile," Bill said.

"That won't be for a while yet."

Bill dismissed the subject with a wave of his hand and strolled away in his socks as Patch called his thanks. Dirk sat down beside Patch. "If another pair of socks would make the shoes fit better, I'll lend you mine."

Patch shook his head and sat with his chin in his hands. After a bit he turned to Dirk. "Mr. Anderson seems to think I *forgot* my shoes."

"Well, didn't you?"

"How could I forget to bring them," Patch asked simply, "when I'm so proud of them?"

"Hmm. Well, what else could have happened?"

"That's what I'd like to know," Patch mumbled, his chin in his hands again.

Dirk shut his eyes on the commotion swirling about him and tried to think—whether this boy, whom actually he knew very slightly, was trying to wriggle out of the blame for his own gross but perhaps excusable oversight —or whether some other member of the team knew and was keeping quiet.

"Let's go back to Thursday afternoon," Dirk said. "I gave you the new shoelaces. Then what did you do?"

41

Patch thought a moment. "You gave me the uniform too."

"Yes. Well, good, tell me every detail."

Patch nodded. "I looked at the uniform first—especially the shirt and its big blue W with wings. I opened my locker and got out this duffel bag you'd issued us earlier and laid the uniform on the bottom. Then I sat down on the floor and took off my shoes and changed the laces."

"Then what?"

"I put the old laces back in the locker. They're still in pretty good shape."

"Okay, okay. And then?"

"I checked all the spikes to see that they were screwed in tight. Then I laid the shoes in the duffel bag and put my sweat suit on top of them. I closed my locker and went to take a shower. Some of the boys were already coming out of the showers by that time."

"You're sure the duffel bag was in the locker and you'd turned the knob on the combination lock?"

"Oh, yes. Nobody took the shoes out of my locker. They were still there after my shower. I know because I took them out of the bag again."

"Oh? Why?"

"I got to worrying that maybe the spikes would poke holes in the new jersey. So I took the shoes out and laid my sweat suit in next and put the shoes on top. Then I zipped up the bag."

"You're positive you put the shoes in again?"

Patch nodded. "I remember that the zipper caught on

42

one of the spikes. So I turned the shoe over and then zipped the bag and put it back in my locker and locked the door."

"Did anyone see you put the shoes back in your bag—anyone who could verify it?"

"Almost everyone had gone home by that time." Patch thought a moment. "Grover! Grover was still there."

"Did he see?"

"His locker is just two down from mine. He could've."

"I'll ask him." Dirk walked over and sat down beside Grover. "Do you know anything about Patch's shoes?" he asked bluntly.

"I do not." Grover glared. "And I resent your question."

"Take is easy, Grover. I worded it wrong and I'm sorry. What I mean is, your locker is near Patch's. After practice Thursday afternoon he was putting things in his duffel bag. Did you happen to notice whether or not he put his shoes in?"

"Thursday after practice," Grover said slowly, apparently reaching back in his memory. He stopped suddenly, and the muscles along his jaw tightened. Dirk, recalling the conversation he had overheard Thursday afternoon, dug nervously at a hangnail along his thumb and waited. Grover opened his palm and looked at a quarter he was holding. He began tossing it back and forth from one hand to the other absently, until a faint smile appeared on his face. He closed his fist over the coin and looked at Dirk.

"Yes, I remember," he said evenly. "It was late. I think

he'd already packed his bag and was reorganizing it. He put the shoes on top, spikes up. I remember thinking, if he sticks his hand in there those spikes will bite him."

"Then what?" Dirk asked.

"He zipped up the bag and put it in his locker."

"Did he lock his locker?"

"I suppose so. I wasn't watching."

"Anything else?"

Grover looked at him strangely. "That's all."

"Well, thanks, Grover. You've told me what I wanted to know."

"Have I now?" Grover asked sardonically, but Dirk scarcely heard him. He was hurrying back to Patch.

"He saw the shoes in your bag. Are you sure that you locked your locker?"

"Positive," Patch said. "I always twirl the knob several times. It was still locked this morning when I went to get the bag."

"Did you look in the bag before we got on the bus?"

"No, but the shoes just had to be in there."

"If they were, then they got as far as the bus." Dirk jumped to his feet. "It's a long shot but I'm going out to the bus and look for them. If some overage prankster—"

"I'm coming along."

Ten minutes later, the search completed, they slumped into seats on the empty bus. The shoes were not there. At that moment Mike Montgomery thrust his head through the open door of the bus.

"Patch!" he shouted. "Get in there! They've called the mile."

Patch leaped up, vaulted out of the bus, and took off for the fieldhouse.

"Holy mother-of-pearl," Mike wailed as he and Dirk trotted after the fast-disappearing Patch. "I've looked all over for that guy. Anderson's about to explode into little pieces."

Chapter 6

When Dirk and Mike lunged into the fieldhouse moments later they saw Patch nearing the track, pulling his sweat shirt over his head as he ran. He tossed it aside and leaped onto the track at the starting line. But the race had already begun, and the other runners were strung out along the backstretch half a lap—one hundred ten yards—away.

The audience gasped as Patch, still wearing his sweat pants, burst onto the track. He angled across to the pole and then drove hard in pursuit of the pack. The spectators started to cheer. Slowly the gap began closing, and the crowd thundered encouragement.

Around the oval came the leaders, the rest of the field trailing along behind. Far last, like a severed tail, came Patch in his sweat pants, still driving hard. The crowd cheered again. Patch heard, and he ran with an open-mouthed smile on his face and a joy that transmitted itself to everyone in the fieldhouse.

Around and around the track the runners circled, Patch drawing ever closer. On his third trip he passed the last laggard. On his fourth lap he passed two more.

On his fifth time around he caught and passed two more runners. Now only six were ahead.

Patch was content to hold his pace on his sixth lap. It carried him gradually closer to the men ahead, until he was almost treading on the heels of the runner in sixth place.

"He'll stay there awhile," Mike Montgomery predicted. "He'll make his move in the last lap."

"Maybe," said Dirk. "That's the way *we'd* do it, if we could. But Patch—I'd hate to predict. This is only his second race. He'll go when the notion strikes him."

It struck him almost at once. He moved into high gear and began overtaking the others, one by one. Coming off the curve into the stretch for the end of his seventh lap, he was third. Now the yelling reached a crescendo. On the straightaway he passed the second man. Three yards farther on he passed the leader. And still the crowd shouted. Patch zipped over the line and started his eighth and last lap a full five yards in the lead. And still the crowd shouted.

Immediately after Patch had passed, a man leaped out from the side line and dashed across the track, holding a string. Two tugs, one from each side of the track, and the tape was taut. The leading runner flung his arms wide, and the broken tape fluttered to the cinders.

Dirk and Mike stared at each other.

"Patch must have missed a lap and a half!" Dirk groaned in dismay. "And he made up only half a lap."

"He doesn't even know it yet. He hasn't looked back."

Two more runners crossed the finish line, and then another.

Patch, on the curve, acknowledged the cheers with a carefree wave of his hand. At that moment the crowd noticed him again and became aware of his error. A few titters rose. Three boys who were standing along the curve hooted and pointed back toward the finish line. Patch looked around over his shoulder, and his stride faltered. All the runners were off the track except a few stragglers who were nearing the finish.

"Now he knows," Dirk said, "poor devil. Just when he thought he had it wrapped up."

Patch's shoulders slumped and his knee-action slowed like a clock running down. The titters spread and massed to a booming guffaw.

Patch raised his head, straightened up, and set out to finish the race. Running alone on an empty track, he regained his stride and moved smoothly along the backstretch. The laughter dwindled and died, merging into applause. He rounded the curve less smoothly, and from time to time his head wobbled a bit. The crowd was standing now and applauding.

"He's pooped," Dirk said. "Ran himself out too early. I only hope he can finish."

Patch came down the homestretch, weariness written on every stride, while the crowd applauded. Two yards from the finish line he stopped, bent his knees, and spread his arms wide.

"What the—?" Dirk began.

Moving along in a squat position, his arms flung out and his body twisting grossly from side to side, Patch duck-waddled across the finish line as the spectators

48

roared with laughter. He crossed the line and flopped on his rear, laughing and sobbing for breath.

"Now I've seen everything," Mike murmured.

"Maybe not," Dirk answered, still not believing what he had seen. "The season is young yet."

It was late that same evening, and Dirk was bone-weary. With a sigh of relief he walked into the coach's office to say good night. Mr. Anderson was leaning back in his desk chair, his hands clasped behind his head.

"The uniforms are all hung up to dry," Dirk said, "and the towels. They'll go in the laundry Monday."

"You," rumbled Anderson, taking his pipe from his mouth, "restore my tottering faith in adolescence."

"Well, thanks. It *has* been kind of a long day, hasn't it? I think I'll go now. Patch is waiting out in the car. I told him I'd take him home."

"Patch. . . ." The coach shook his head. "It's a cruel thing when a man of my age and experience—a man who can turn a fine phrase or chop a man down with a word—can't think of a thing to say to a teen-ager."

"To Patch?" Dirk asked meekly.

"To Patch." Mr. Anderson sighed. "He comes puffing up to me after the race too winded to talk. I propose to tell him I'm not an animal trainer, not even of sleek intelligent seals and never of waddling ducks. But the kid is so happy he's bursting, and some of it rubs off on me."

He knocked the ashes out of his pipe, and Dirk waited.

"So I think I'll tell him it was good that he didn't quit, however silly he must have felt, stranded out there alone on the track. But blast it, he should have been there at the start, and then he'd never have been left over, alone like an echo. I'm ready to eat him alive for showing up missing."

He refilled his pipe and poked at the tobacco furiously. "And then I remember the stop watch. I clocked him, you know." He halted and glared at Dirk. "No, you wouldn't," he grumbled. "I clocked him in 4:32, including the last two yards of whatever it was. Think of it, boy! Look impressed! If the meet had been held in Crescent City, that would have been a new city record. Officially, of course, the time starts with the gun. But on a strange track, an indoor track, in somebody else's shoes—"

He laid down his pipe and slumped forward on one elbow. "Shoes. . . . After all," he asked softly, "what are shoes to a runner? So he comes off and leaves them behind. Gah. . . . And he stands there huffing and puffing and panting before me, grinning from ear to ear like a duck."

He raised his hand before Dirk could protest. "Ducks *do* grin. Look at the next duck you see—any duck except Donald. . . . And he stands there before me grinning and waiting, and what does the great man say? . . . He says nothing."

His booming voice ceased, and silence seeped in and crowded the tiny room.

The coach leaned back in his chair, chuckling. "Your turn," he said, propping his feet on the desk.

"Well—" Dirk cleared his throat. "I hardly know where to begin."

Anderson nodded. "I'm glad I made my point—so concisely."

"About the 4:32," Dirk said, "that's swell. I'm not sure he could do it again. The circumstances—"

"—won't be repeated, I hope."

"And the shoes. The borrowed shoes didn't bother him much. They were only a size too large. I asked him about them after the race, and he said he hadn't noticed."

"Better if they'd given him fits. Then he'd remember his own."

"But Mr. Anderson, Patch didn't forget his shoes! He remembers every detail about putting them in. He's fallen in love with those track shoes."

Anderson looked at him quizzically.

"Grover remembers too," Dirk added. "Grover saw them in Patch's bag."

Anderson's feet came down with a thud. "When?" he asked.

"Last thing Thursday afternoon."

The big man swiveled around in his chair and sat staring out the window. A full minute passed before he swung back. "You say Patch is waiting in your car?"

Dirk nodded.

"Call him in and tell him to open his locker."

The metal door swung back with a creak that resounded through the silent locker room.

"I opened it when we got back tonight," Patch was saying, "and put my bag up here on the top shelf. There's nothing else in here except that towel." He indicated a crumpled, soiled towel lying at the bottom of the locker.

Dirk turned to the coach with a feeling of vindication.

Mr. Anderson was frowning into the locker. He leaned over and lifted the towel. A pair of track shoes lay underneath it.

Dirk stared. He became aware of Patch at his elbow staring too.

"There's the end of your mystery, boys," Mr. Anderson said.

Dirk shook his head. "No, Mr. Anderson. This is just the beginning. Why did Grover say that he saw them in Patch's bag?"

"Because he did," Patch answered with simple logic. "They were in my bag—and then they weren't."

Chapter 7

Standing together on the practice field the following Thursday afternoon, burly, blond muscle-man Moose Elliot and small, dark wire-taut Benny Chapnik looked like father and son. But it was Benny who was holding forth like a father—or volunteer coach.

"With a build like yours," Benny was saying, "your opportunities are immense."

"Like *me*," Moose said. "Well, I *am* a pretty fair guard."

"I mean in track."

"Track?" asked Moose as if hearing the word for the first time. "Never once gave it a thought till somebody wrote a new rule: No more spring football practice. The football coach didn't like that a bit. He said, 'You want to play on my team in the fall, you go out for track in the spring and get yourselves in condition.' So here I am, pushing around what Patch called the iron ball."

"Could be," mused Benny, "that you have a greater future in track than in football."

"Ha!" Moose answered eloquently.

"Football stars might make a few trips to the coast," said Benny, "but track stars travel all over the world."

"How come?"

"Exhibitions and the Olympics."

"Can't but three American shot-putters make the Olympics."

"That gives you three chances."

Moose flipped the twelve-pound shot into his other hand. "Pushing this ball is work enough without trying to push my luck too."

Benny ignored it. "Size you already have, the size of the world's best. Other athletes, you know, call shot-putters 'whales.' But never 'meese.'"

"Meese?"

"Or do you say 'mooses'? This English!" He spread his hands. "Well, I was saying. . . . Power you already have. You need only to make it work for you."

"Yeah, wouldn't that be nice?"

"It's quite within your control."

"It is?"

"Work! Parry O'Brien, the Olympic champion, worked seven years, sometimes putting the shot as often as a hundred and fifty times a day. He said, and I've read this: 'I don't quit until my hands are bleeding, and that's the god's truth.'" *

Moose looked at his upturned palms. "For what?"

"But of course—for perfection."

"You mean there's no easier way?"

* Aspiring shot-putters will find Joel Sayre's article "Parry's Power of Positive Thought" in *Sports Illustrated* for March 21, 1955, both interesting and instructive.

"There are other things that will help. What do you do before you compete—just before you step into the circle?"

"Oh, a few warm-ups—if Anderson's looking."

"O'Brien says that the secret is getting keyed up—he says 'to a point where everything about you is so taut it might break.' Get nervous, he says. Make your heart pound like a trip hammer. Think yourself into a frenzy."

"Gawsh, how d'you do *that?*"

"He did it through yoga and primitive music and concentration. When he's ready for a toss, he says, he's all wrapped up in himself. He's in a different world. 'I work myself up to such a pitch,' he says, 'that finally, when I reach for the shot, it feels like three pounds. Then when I heave it, I'm better than I really am. Like a crazy man . . .'"

Moose shook his head slowly. "For me to try to drive myself crazy, I'd have to be crazy to start with."

"Try it just once, won't you, Moose? Try it this Saturday in our first meet?"

Moose looked down at the eager face. "Well . . . what have I got to lose—but my mind?" He shrugged his huge shoulders. "I'm not sure why," he said with a slow smile, "but I'll try it."

"Now where," Mr. Anderson asked Dirk, "are our three milers?"

"Benny is giving Moose some advice," Dirk said. "Patch is doing a lap with the 440 boys. And Grover is over there on the rail—"

"With the good-looking girl. Some day you'll learn,

Dirk, that all track athletes are prima donnas." He blew a great blast on his whistle and motioned the three boys to him.

When they had gathered around, he said, "Day after tomorrow is our first regular meet, and we have a bit of planning to do."

"Planning what?" Patch asked blithely.

"The race, Ducky," answered Grover. "Maybe it's news to you—and I'm sure it is—but the mile is a race of strategy."

The coach smiled. "Somewhat brutally put, Grover, but nonetheless true. The mile is a head-to-foot proposition, the mind reviewing the strategy planned in advance, holding rein on the feet, observing the opposition, and watching for chances."

"All that and running too," murmured Patch.

"You have to concentrate, Patch," Mr. Anderson said. "When you're running the mile, you have to *think*."

"Oh, I do. When I'm out there running the mile, I'm thinking every second. Maybe not about the race, but I'm thinking."

The coach looked as if he wanted to laugh and cry at the same time. "First," he continued after a moment, "know yourself and then your opponents. What *you* can do and what *they* can do."

"How do you find out?" Patch asked.

"About your opponents? It isn't easy before the first meet. Judging from last year's varsities and the boys coming up from the freshman teams—allowing of course for improvement—the mile strength in Crescent City this year seems to be centered in Lincoln and East."

"And West," added Benny.

Mr. Anderson nodded. "I hope so."

"You mean, sir," asked Benny, "that when we meet Central and North in the triangular meet this Saturday, the milers will be—"

"So-so. It looks that way, Benny, but I don't know. With luck we might make a clean sweep—but not if you run with your feet alone. Last Saturday, Patch—"

Patch looked sheepish.

"Last Saturday I didn't think you'd be able to finish. You'll have to start slower, conserve—"

"But golly, Mr. Anderson. I start down the track and I get so excited, I just want to keep going faster!"

"After a month of pace work, you still can't gauge pace. Some day a coach will send a boy out there and tell him to run you out of your shoes. At the end of the first half-mile you'll be pooped. And while you're wobbling and wondering if you can lift your knees just once more, some other boy will step past you and go on to win."

Patch grinned. "Short race and a merry one."

"Gah. Fall for that and we'll *see* who's merry. But we're not taking any chances. Grover will set the pace. You follow two or three strides behind, off his outside shoulder, till the end of the third lap. You're on your own after that. But even after you've passed Grover, gauge your strength and save your finishing kick. You'll accelerate only once. Wait till you know you can hold the faster pace all the way to the tape."

He turned to Benny. "I don't know yet how fast you can go the distance. In the tryouts last month the time

57

for the mile was 5:05, and you were fifteen yards out at the finish. I think you've improved a good bit since then. Do you think you're, say, ten seconds faster?"

Benny nodded.

"Do you want to be paced," the coach asked, "or run on your own?"

"On my own."

"With his faithful clock in his hot little hand," Grover murmured under his breath.

"Then try to take each of the first three quarters in seventy-four," Mr. Anderson told Benny. "On the last lap you can hold the same pace for a 4:56 mile or try to speed up, depending on what you have left. I don't even know if you've got a kick. If you have, save it. Save it till you come off the last curve—unless you have to turn it on sooner to stay within striking distance."

Benny nodded again.

"And me?" Grover asked, looking sullen.

"You set the pace for Patch. Get away fast and try for the pole. Then settle down into a steady pace. Hold it for three laps. After that, you're on your own to do what you can in the last lap. The main thing is, you set the pace."

Grover studied his fingernails. "Name it," he said non-committally.

Mr. Anderson fiddled with his whistle a moment, then let it fall on his chest. "I think a 4:50 mile will win this one. That's pretty fair time this early. But we'll figure on 4:46 to be safe. Take the first three laps in seventy-two seconds each. That's 3:36 for three quarters. Patch, you ought to be able to do the last lap in seventy seconds for a 4:46 mile. At the end of three laps, Grover, you give Patch the signal to pass."

Grover's face became blotchy with anger. "I'm to play fall guy?"

"Fall guy? How do you figure?"

"You know as well as I do that the fellow who sets the pace is a sitting duck for someone who finishes fast. They just lay behind and let *him* do the work, and then in the last few yards they zip past him and win."

Mr. Anderson shrugged. "You're on your own for the last lap, remember. Go as fast as you like."

"That's just it! I run a good steady race. Four quarters in, say, seventy-two for a 4:48 mile. Four quarters of equal time—that's the proper way."

"Hmmm. If you'd listened to me when I talked about form, you'd have enough energy left at the end for a finishing kick, and then you'd consider it smart to close fast. As it is, you don't even run four equal quarters. You always start dragging a bit toward the last."

"See! That proves it. You're trying to rig this and make me the fall guy so your playboy can win. You know I can't overtake him, once he goes past."

Under his mop of gray hair, the coach's forehead turned fiery red.

"Besides," Grover continued, "what about seniority? I'm a letter-man. City champion! I should have someone setting the pace for me!"

Coach Anderson thrust his grizzled head forward and opened his mouth, but Benny spoke first.

"I'll set the pace."

Grover turned. From his six-feet-one he looked disdainfully down on Benny, who was stretched to his full five-seven.

"You and your stop watch," Grover scoffed. "You and your Nurmi shuffle. A pacemaker has to have speed." He turned to Patch. "And 'a pacemaker has to know pace." He looked at the coach. "When it comes to qualifications, you're right. I'm your man. And since you think I'm expendable, I'll set the pace and wave to your playboy to come on past me and win. But I'm asking for a gentleman's agreement. If he doesn't win this time, we'll write the experiment off as a flop."

Chapter 8

It was topcoat weather and the stadium at North High was less than half filled, but the feel of spring was in the air that early-April afternoon. This was the day for a track meet—calm and crisp under a bright blue sky. Dirk felt again the tingle of excitement that he always felt at a track meet. Watching the events, he put aside thoughts of towels and tape and equipment and reveled in the sheer beauty of the most graceful of sports.

The guarded voice beside him was Mr. Anderson's. "What," the coach was asking, "has come over our Moose?"

Moose was pacing up and down beside the shot-put circle, clenching and unclenching his fists and shaking his head.

"Once such a stolid citizen," Mr. Anderson murmured.

Moose stopped, but his lips started moving and his eyes had a faraway look.

"Coach," whispered Dirk, "I think that's yoga."

Anderson shot him a bleak glance. "Even the manager's gone mad."

At that moment Moose moved his massive hulk into

the circle. He flipped the iron ball back and forth in his hands. He took a huge breath. He leaned over and squeezed his eyes shut, and his lips moved again. Then he whirled and slammed his foot forward. Muscles bulging, he brought his body and arm forward in a mighty heave. The shot flew out into space.

Mr. Anderson's eyes grew larger and larger as they followed its trajectory. When the shot thudded to earth, he strode over and gripped Moose's hand.

"I don't need a tape measure to tell me that this is by far the best put you've ever made."

Moose opened his eyes and looked. "Geez, it worked!" His face broke open in a smile. "Thanks, Mr. Anderson." He drew his arm across his dripping forehead. "The fellow who really did that was Benny Chapnik."

The milers, nine of them, were prancing about at the starting line. Now they halted and stood in their lanes as the official starter stepped into position. Grover was dour and alert, moving his eyes without moving his head. Patch was staring across the field, watching the progress of the high jump in its early stages. Benny was raising a small plastic bottle to his lips. He took a gulp, screwed the cap on, and handed the bottle to Dirk.

"Would you mind holding this, please, Dirk?"

"What is it?" Dirk asked, turning the bottle and watching the amber fluid move sluggishly.

"Liquid honey—for energy."

"Something you've read, no doubt?" Dirk asked, smiling. "Well, keep up your reading, Benny. You just got Moose a first in the shot-put."

Benny looked pleased. "I only wish it would work for me. But runners are supposed to relax, and who can relax in a race?"

Dirk glanced across to the third lane, where Grover was standing. "Grover!" Dirk called. "You remember?"

Grover nodded grimly.

"Take your marks!" the starter shouted, raising the pistol.

Dirk moved out of the way. A few seconds later he was standing along the side line with Mr. Anderson when the runners took off.

Grover shot to the front and laid claim to the pole position. In the quick reshuffling, Patch and Benny were lost to view for a moment. Patch emerged soon to fall into third place three strides behind Grover, between them a Central boy in a gold jersey. Benny seemed content to stay with the pack.

On the backstretch Patch was second. The Central boy had not held the pace and had dropped back from second to fourth. Grover was eating the ground with enormous strides, running too far up on his toes, knees flashing high.

With an effort Dirk choked back his favorite comment, that here was the prettiest runner of all, the perfect picture of grace and form. Patch, by contrast, took shorter strides and just seemed somehow to float along without effort. And Benny, pale and colorless, really did look to be shuffling along scarcely lifting his knees. You had to watch closely to see that he wasn't quite running flat-footed.

"Benny better get moving!" Dirk muttered. "He's already thirty yards back, even though he *is* running third."

Coach Anderson looked at his stop watch and frowned and said nothing.

Grover and Patch came pounding around the curve and down the straight stretch. As they swept past the starting line, Coach Anderson leaned out over the track.

"Slow down!" he shouted. "Slow down!"

Grover swept past unhearing. Patch turned his head, looked puzzled, wavered a second, and then continued at Grover's pace and at his flying heels.

Much later—fifty-five yards behind them—Benny came past the starting line. Dirk saw him glance at his stop watch as he finished the first lap. Behind Benny the rest of the field was well strung out down the stretch, and several runners were still on the curve. Grover had already entered the opposite curve.

"That Grover," Coach Anderson sputtered, "I'll have his hide. He can't possibly keep this up for a mile, and neither can Patch."

"Keep what up?"

"Grover's running at his top speed for the 880!"

"Whew! You think he knows it?"

"Sure he knows. For all his faults, that boy's a fine judge of pace."

"Then why—?"

The coach shook his head. "Can't imagine. . . . Well, yes I can. Setting a sizzling early pace is a way to drain off the strength of a fast finisher so he can't summon up that final burst."

64

"Aw, you don't do that to a teammate. And how about Benny?"

"Didn't bite. He hit his seventy-four on the button."

"Well, anyhow, there's no competition. Look at them, Coach. Have you ever seen a crazier race?"

On the second lap Grover already was nearing the end of the backstretch. Patch was three strides behind. Benny, in third, was lagging now by some ninety yards. He was at the other end of the backstretch, trailed by the Central boy, who apparently had decided to let the two fly-boys go and had fastened on Benny as pacemaker. Even these two were far ahead of the rest of the field.

"When they come past us this time," Mr. Anderson was saying, "I'm going to concentrate on Patch. Let Grover knock himself out if he wants to. Patch has to be told."

He leaned forward and glared down the stretch as Grover and Patch approached. Dirk leaned out too, waiting for the moment when Patch was almost opposite them.

At the precise moment, both yelled in unison.

"Patch! Slow down! Let Grover go on," Mr. Anderson shouted.

"Patch! Don't try to keep up with Grover," Dirk yelled.

As the jumbled words reached him, Patch turned a startled face to the side line. "What?" he called back over his shoulder.

Again the two shouted together, and again the words drowned one another. Patch, well down the track by this time, looked back and shook his head and kept going.

The coach whirled on Dirk. "*You* were a big help."

"Oh, gosh, I guess he didn't hear us, did he?"

"I guess you can't imagine why," Mr. Anderson snorted. He glanced at the stop watch. "Missed the time too," he grumbled. "I think it was—" He shook his head in disbelief. "Must have been about 2:10 for the 880. One of Grover's better times for that distance."

"How long can he keep it up?"

"Not even this long, I'd have told you a minute ago."

Midway of the backstretch on his third lap Grover was beginning to tire. Patch was still following at his heels. The rest of the backstretch was empty, as was the south curve. After this huge gap came Benny, 135 yards behind, just entering the south curve. The others followed at varying distances along the straight stretch in front of the stands. Some had not yet started their third lap.

Across the field Grover was motioning for Patch to pass, and Patch went around. Grover wobbled a few yards farther, stepped off the track, and dropped to his hands and knees on the grass.

"Gah," grumbled Anderson. "There goes our clean sweep."

Patch appeared at the head of the stretch a few seconds later, still running strongly. Mr. Anderson leaned out, then pulled his head back to face Dirk.

"*You* shut up!" he told Dirk and thrust the stop watch into Dirk's hand. "Here. Get his time."

As Patch came closer the coach cupped his hands and

shouted distinctly, "Slow down! . . . Float. . . . Take it easy!"

This time Patch nodded and grinned and slowed down.

"Jeest!" said Dirk, staring at the stop watch. "Three-twenty for three quarters."

Coach Anderson nodded. "About what I figured. He slowed down when Grover slowed down, just before he dropped out. Then Patch kept on at the slower pace. Not that seventy seconds flat is slow for a quarter."

"You think he can finish?"

"Maybe. Now. There's a lot of strength in that compact frame."

"I'll say. Did you know that he ran a block at top speed from the bus to the fieldhouse just before he ran the mile in the State Relays?"

Mr. Anderson raised his eyebrows. "All the same, I'm thankful that this is his last lap."

"He could almost walk it and win, the others are so far behind."

Patch at that moment was once again on the back-stretch, and the other seven nearly covered the track.

"No telling how many runners he'll lap," Mr. Anderson said. "Poorest crop of milers I've seen in many a day. No speed, and most of them aren't in shape for the distance yet."

Patch glided around the curve in his easy stride and entered the homestretch. He passed two fading runners and was closing in fast on a third. Dirk leaned forward and peered down the stretch.

"The kid looks downright happy. None of that tortured look of a runner in trouble. They'd better start stretching the tape. He'll finish for sure."

Patch passed a third man and came on fast, looking ahead for the tape. There was no tape across the track. Consternation swept his face as he crossed the finish line.

Coach Anderson clicked the stop watch and leaned over it eagerly. "A 4:28!" he gloated. "Fastest mile ever run by a high school boy in Crescent City. Faster by almost ten seconds. This puts him right up among the best in the state. Oh, have I got me a miler now!" He was almost dancing with glee.

He turned to Dirk. "Soon as he's walked around a bit, I want to tell him so." He looked about. "Say, where is he?"

"There!" Dirk pointed to a slight figure chugging around the far curve.

Anderson looked and groaned. "Why? Why in tarnation is the gloop running a fifth lap? And don't dare tell me it's because he likes to run."

Dirk shook his head. "There wasn't any tape."

"Of course not. Three runners hadn't finished the third lap yet."

"I guess he figured—*no tape, so the race isn't over, I must have miscounted*—and just kept going."

"Here comes Benny. Blast it, I've shut off the watch."

Benny was finishing fast to beat out his erstwhile shadow, the Central boy, by ten yards. Dirk hailed Benny with a joyous shout as he crossed the line, and a smile flickered across Benny's thin, tense face. A North runner's finishing kick was too late by five yards to gain him third place. Across the field the other four runners

68

were weaving as they followed Patch, who was still going strong.

At that moment Grover reappeared.

"Coach," he said, puffing, "I hurried over as soon as I could to explain."

Mr. Anderson, hands on his hips, looked Grover over. "I'm waiting."

"I got mixed up," Grover said, his chest still heaving. "I thought I was running the 880."

Mr. Anderson's face was inscrutable. "One way or another, I'll agree," he said coldly, "that you got mixed up. Well, it's nobody's funeral but your own. Patch set a new record, thanks to you. And Benny will take home a shiny red ribbon that might have been yours."

Chapter 9

Sax Warner sat in the journalism office Monday nibbling the end of his pencil.

"Subtle," he said to Grover. "It's got to be subtle."

"Consider your readers, Sax. We'll make it just subtle enough that the sports editor won't blue-pencil it."

"Consider my by-line, you mean. This column comes out with my name above it. That makes a writer think twice. It isn't just something they read in the paper. It's something Sax Warner said."

"Uh-huh. Only this time it'll be something Grover Godwin said and Sax Warner put down on paper under his by-line."

"Provided Sax Warner likes it."

"He'll like it," Grover snapped.

Sax bristled.

"All I want," Grover said quickly, "is to make Patch look silly."

"Sort of—returning the favor?"

Grover flushed. "For that crack you can start out like this: 'Grover Godwin, champion miler, led all the way till a leg cramp forced him out of the race in the third lap.' "

"Leg cramp, my foot. You were pooped." Sax finished writing the sentence and laid down his pencil. "What ever possessed you to whirl around the track like a dashman?"

"I was setting the pace for Patch. On Anderson's orders."

"*That* pace?"

Grover shrugged. "Maybe I misjudged a little."

"Maybe you misjudged a lot. But it wasn't the pace you misjudged; it was Patch. You knew exactly what you were doing."

"I usually *do*," Grover said smugly.

Sax twirled his pencil and smiled. "The kid sure made you look foolish. Just between us, he's fabulous, isn't he? Finishing five laps before some of the twerps had run four, and finishing fresher."

"It's bad for morale," Grover said. "Bad for the morale of the boys who were lapped—"

"Not that you've ever lost sleep over the morale of opponents."

"—and bad for the morale of his own running mates, however good they might be."

"I have a sneaking suspicion," said Sax, "that it's harder on Godwin than Chapnik."

"Chapnik!" grunted Grover. "You know what that pipsqueak told me after the race? He said, 'There is an historical precedent for your feat.' You know how he talks, with that accent. 'An historical precedent,' he said, 'that should have forewarned you.' "

"Yeah?"

"That's what I said. And he told me that in 1945 Arne Anderson tried to run Gunder the Wonder Hägg off his feet. This Gunder's a fast finisher, it seems, and Arne wanted to drain off his zip."

"What happened?"

"Gunder the Wonder set a new world record."

"Say, I'll use that in my column! Neat coincidence."

Grover looked at Sax coldly and steadily a long time before answering. Finally he murmured, "Use it—and Anderson will hear about a certain matter that's been troubling me for days, much as I hate to pigeon on a teammate—it says here in fine print."

Sax stirred uneasily, scowled, and picked up his pencil. "Okay, okay, I've got this about Grover Godwin, champion miler, getting a leg cramp. You sure that's the way you want it? 'Champion miler'? Not 'Glitter-Boy Grover'? Not 'handsome' Grover? Not 'picture-runner'?"

"Everyone knows that already."

"Anderson doesn't. And how about Benny? Seems to me he's made some suggestions. Wants you to use the European style, doesn't he? Says all the great milers use it. Not running so high on your toes, less knee lift, shorter stride—"

"That's a *little* man talking."

"Well, let's get on with the column. You had something you wanted to say about Patch. What was it?"

Grover put his fingertips together carefully. "Your TRACK TALK is a column of odds-and-ends . . ."

"You could call it that. Comments, opinions, inside information from a track man. . . . The straight news story on each meet is handled separately, usually by the sports editor."

"Okay, so the editor tells about Patch winning. You just put in a comment about him. The article makes him look like a great man. You come along and in a few well-chosen words make him look like a stupe."

"Under my by-line, remember. What are the well-chosen words?"

"Try this." Grover leaned back and dictated slowly, as if he were seeing the item as it would appear in print in the school paper.

I was reading not long ago about the Australian aborigines, primitive tribesmen who never have learned to cook their food. Even today they hunt with a spear because they've never invented the bow and arrow. Rumor has it, they don't know what causes babies. And they still haven't learned to count. Most of them can count up to two. A few can count as high as four, but the word for five means "many."

Coach Anderson now has unveiled our own West High aborigine. On two successive Saturdays, Aboriginal Jones has demonstrated that *he* hasn't learned to count yet either.

Wednesday morning in homeroom Miss Murdock passed out the school newspapers and settled down at her desk with a sigh of relief as her junior homeroom bent over their papers in silence. She noted with mild disapproval that the boys turned first to the sports page

73

instead of the news or editorial, but soon she found herself doing the same. She read about Aboriginal Jones and looked up to see his sandy head bent quietly over his paper. He was reading the right-hand column, the account of the meet, and smiling.

Somebody snickered. She saw a boy elbow his neighbor and point to Sax Warner's column. They both looked at Patch and snickered. From the other side of the room came an answering snicker.

Soon a girl tittered and pointed at Patch. Two other girls put their heads together and giggled and kept peering back over their shoulders at the mercifully oblivious Patch, who still read on.

Moose Elliot suddenly threw back his head and roared with laughter. Every head in the room snapped up. Miss Murdock pushed back her chair and stood, ready to bring the situation under control.

"What's so funny?" somebody asked.

"This thing about Patch," Moose said. He held up his paper and pointed. The heads went down again, reading. Patch's stayed down the longest. His neck turned red, a fact that a classmate carefully pointed out to the others behind Patch. Smothered laughter and the sibilant sounds of suppressed amusement drifted about. As the tittering rose, Miss Murdock opened her mouth to call a halt. At that moment the bell clanged, ending the homeroom period.

The students pushed noisily to the door, only Patch, Moose, and Miss Murdock lingering. From the hall outside came a jeering horselaugh. Miss Murdock gathered

her books, pondering the thoughtless brutality of adolescence, and followed Moose and Patch into the hall.

In the seething throng, heads turned at the sight of
Patch—and turned quickly away to the sound of smothered laughter. Miss Murdock looked at Patch's blue eyes,
empty for the first time of the laughter that always lay
behind them.

Moose clapped Patch on the shoulder. "Aboriginal
Jones!" he roared. "How many fingers?" Moose raised
his big hand, fingers spread.

Patch grinned foolishly. He leaned forward and stared
at the fingers, and the twinkle suddenly reappeared in
his eyes. He reached out and touched the hand tenta-
tively with his fingertips, as other students gathered
around to watch.

"How many fingers?" Moose repeated. The other students pushed closer, snickering and nudging one another.

"How many fingers?"

Patch cleared his throat. In a voice that quavered he
asked, "Many?"

The hall rang with laughter.

Moose clapped Patch on the shoulder again. "That's
our boy!" he shouted gaily.

The others echoed his words. They crowded around,
patting Patch on the shoulder, calling him their boy,
and holding up five fingers. Then they wandered away
down the hall saying, "Many," flashing five fingers at one
another, and laughing and murmuring, "What a guy!"

Miss Murdock turned away with a sigh. "I guess we'll

be hearing that all day now." She chuckled. "How many fingers? . . . Many!" She passed the great Grover Godwin, strangely bleak in this sea of good will, but even his obvious ill-humor did not dampen her joy. She was still smiling broadly when she entered her classroom, and her students noted with satisfaction that teacher was in a good humor today.

Chapter 10

Dirk nosed his ancient sedan out of the driveway and headed for school. "Sure, it's too early to be out of your stall, Little Otto," he said, patting the steering wheel. "Six forty-five. But tomorrow's Saturday, so you can stay in the garage till noon."

He drove along sleepy-eyed and yawning, grumbling about his own carelessness. "My one-track mind. I was so intent on distributing the clean uniforms for tomorrow's meet, Little Otto, that I clear forgot to bring in the equipment after practice yesterday." As he was talking he hit a chuckhole, and the car bounced and groaned. "Have your say, Little Otto," Dirk rambled on. "It's nothing to what Mr. Anderson would tell me if he got to school before I did and saw those things still out on the field."

He drove quickly along the empty road and through the streets of the sleeping city. It was not quite seven o'clock when he drew up behind the school, which had never looked so deserted. His was the first car. He parked and started to walk down the stadium steps.

Out on the field a figure was running around the oval.

Now and then the boy glanced at something he held in his hand, and Dirk knew that the runner was Benny. I'll wait on the steps till he's finished the quarter, Dirk thought, but Benny kept going for two more laps. Then he pulled up, jotted something on a slip of paper, and started jogging wearily toward the steps.

"Hi, Benny," Dirk called, going on down as Benny was starting up. Benny raised his head, startled. He was breathing heavily.

"Postman's holiday?" Dirk asked. "I thought the day before a meet was a day of rest."

"Supposed to be," Benny panted. "Mr. Anderson wouldn't approve," he acknowledged guiltily.

"He wouldn't approve of what I'm doing either," Dirk said. "I forgot to take in the stuff last night."

"I'll help you."

Ten minutes later they had finished, and Benny was saying, "I'll have to get home now so I can shower and change clothes and eat breakfast and get back to school by eight."

Dirk watched him start for the steps. "Thanks a lot, Ben."

Benny stopped with his hand on the rail and turned around. "Have you had breakfast?"

"Well, no. I left home too early. But I thought I might pick up something here in the cafeteria—"

"Why don't you come home and have breakfast with me?"

"Here we are," Benny said.

Dirk braked his car in front of a lean, gray, tired-looking frame house. They walked around to the back door and entered the kitchen, and the scent and sound of bubbling coffee greeted them at the door.

A wiry little woman looked up from the stove in surprise.

"Mother," said Benny, "this is Dirk Ingersoll, a friend of mine. I've asked him to have breakfast with us."

She came forward and held out both hands to Dirk. "Thiss iss verrry nice!"

Dirk wavered between the two hands and finally grasped both of them. "How do you do, Mrs. Chapnik," he said. "I know this is an imposition—"

She answered quickly, but Dirk couldn't understand.

"She's glad that you've come," Benny interpreted. "She likes to meet my friends, and I bring them so seldom. . . . You'll probably have trouble understanding Mama. She doesn't get so much practice in English as Papa and I do. So why don't you go into the living room and sit down? I'll be dressed in about ten minutes. Breakfast will be ready by then."

In ten minutes Benny was back. Together they strolled into the kitchen, where breakfast for four lay steaming on the table. A short, brisk, heavily-muscled man strode in, and Dirk was introduced to Mr. Chapnik as they all sat down at the small table.

"You go to the high school with Benjy?" Mr. Chapnik asked. His accent, though much more marked than Benny's, was understandable.

Dirk nodded, his mouth full of food.

"I was a high school teacher myself in Europe," said Mr. Chapnik, "though it was not called 'high school' in our country."

"What country was that?" Dirk asked.

"Latvia."

Silence hung over the table a moment before Mrs. Chapnik spoke. Slowly, as if groping for words, she said, "Benjy duss not remember de country where he wass born."

"I remember our house," said Benny. "I remember the sea—the Baltic. After all, I was almost four when we left."

"It wass not de same, not rilly our country."

Mr. Chapnik explained. "The Russian troops came in '39. They stayed and took over. That was before Benjy was born. In '41, German troops came and drove the Russians away; and the Germans stayed. But the Russians came back after several years. We fought them. Alongside the Germans we fought them, but the Russians were far too strong for us. It was October of '44 that Riga, our capital, fell. Then Manya and Benjy and I lost no time leaving the country."

"I cried," Benny said. "I didn't want to go."

"Benjy howled," Mr. Chapnik said, "just when we wanted most to be inconspicuous."

"I wanted to take everything," Benny added, "all that we owned. But everything that we took we had to carry."

"Where did you go?" Dirk asked.

"To western Germany."

"Germany!" Dirk said, eyes bugging. "You were put in a concentration camp?"

Mr. Chapnik shook his head. "Thousands of Latvians fled into Germany. Thousands of people from all over eastern Europe fled westward before the oncoming Russians."

"Where did they all go?"

"Most, I think, went to Germany."

Dirk was quiet a moment, thinking of tales his father had told him.

"My dad was a bombardier," Dirk said. "He was stationed in England then—'44 and '45. He's told me about the bombing of Germany, how American planes—great fleets of them—took off at dawn each day and bombed the devil out of Germany, month in and month out. And British bombers were doing the same each night. *You* were living in Germany then?"

Mr. Chapnik nodded. "By choice." He smiled at Dirk's consternation. "My boy, there are worse things than bombs."

They went on eating. Dirk did not answer immediately, but he was curious to hear the rest of the story. "After the war," he asked, "where did you go?"

"We stayed in Germany," Mr. Chapnik said. "We couldn't go back. Nothing had changed. The Russians are still there."

"We were eager to go somewhere else," Benny added. "The Germans had scarcely enough to live on themselves, and so many had lost their homes by bombing. We had descended on them like the locusts, thousands of homeless foreigners. We must have been an almost intolerable burden. But where could we go?"

"Over here?" Dirk asked.

"America," Mr. Chapnik said, "was the country everyone dreamed of. An impossibly wonderful land. An unattainable dreamland. Of course we tried. We tried for five years. But it seemed hopeless."

"You lived in Germany five years?"

"Nearly seven years," Benny answered. "And then we almost went to Australia. Arrangements were made—in '51—for a large group of refugees in our part of Germany to be sent to Australia, and we were to be among them. Weeks passed, and we waited. One day Papa went off to another town looking for odd jobs. That same day the word came through; we were to leave at once. Before we could reach Papa, the others left. So we stayed on in Germany, wondering if we had missed our last chance. It was only two months after that that we got this chance to come to America, a chance we had almost missed."

"Over here," Mr. Chapnik said, "we applied for naturalization. And after we had lived in this country five years—the waiting period required by law—we appeared in naturalization court for our final hearing and passed the examination."

"You'd be surprised," Benny put in, "how much the so-called foreigners are required to know about the American government."

Mr. Chapnik smiled and waved the matter aside. "So we are truly Americans now. And we know—better than *most* Americans know—how lucky we are!"

"That's quite true and Papa's favorite subject," said Benny, pushing back his chair, "but if you've finished,

Dirk, we must be getting back to school right away."

"So that's how you got here," Dirk mused as they drove along. The street was crowded with cars now, and traffic was slow.

"It was one of my two boyhood dreams." Benny smiled. "All boys have dreams. Sometimes they only dream of owning a Cadillac. Or maybe an island all their own."

"What was your other dream?"

Benny looked slightly embarrassed, and Dirk was about to withdraw the question when Benny spoke up abruptly. "An Olympic gold medal!"

"Wow."

"Yes, I thought so too once. To be the best in the world—as impossible as my first dream. It wasn't until the last Olympics that I re-examined it seriously and weighed my chances. I knew that I'd never jump seven feet or put the shot sixty-two. I could never, no matter how long I practiced, run the hundred in 9.3. I have, in fact, very little of what is called natural ability."

"Yeah, well, that *would* sort of enter the picture."

"But not so much in the mile, where proficiency comes with persistence. I've read everything I could find about the great distance runners, and every article says the same thing. Run! Paavo Nurmi ran five miles to and from work every day. Kitei Son, the Japanese who won the Olympic marathon in 1936, had worked for years as a rickshaw boy. Over here, Wes Santee rounded up cattle on foot."

Dirk thought about Patch running home from the Millville school, five miles, and running across the hills to wave at a passing train.

"You can do it in formal practice too," Benny said as if reading Dirk's thoughts. "Zapotek, the Czech who set three new Olympic records at Helsinki in '52, once ran sixty quarters in a single workout—and ran each quarter in sixty seconds. Roger Bannister of England, first man to break the four-minute mile, prepared for it by training several times a week, each time running ten consecutive quarter-miles at the same speed. He started in December, running the quarters in sixty-six seconds. By April he had brought the time down to fifty-nine."

"Consecutive quarters, you said. You mean all at once?"

"An interval of about two minutes between each quarter. I'm trying to do it *his* way, except that I run five mornings each week."

"Oh?"

"I started in January, and I'd rather not tell you how slow my time was those first few weeks. Not that it's fast after running each morning for three and a half months. But that's all right. I expected slow progress. The one thing I've been learning all my life is patience."

"Where do you run?"

"At school on the track—very early. During the winter I even ran in the snow if it wasn't too deep."

Dirk burst out laughing, and Benny seemed to shrivel a little.

"Sorry, Benny. I was thinking about the snowmen."

"Snowmen?"

84

"Have you ever heard of the legendary snowmen of the Himalayan mountains? Nobody knows what they are, but high up on the mountains, far above the tree line, far above food, they leave their mysterious footprints in the snow. This winter we thought we had a snowman here at West. After every snow we saw footprints around the track, no matter how early we came to school or how late at night the snow had fallen."

Benny nodded and smiled. "My footprints."

They had reached the school, and Dirk swung into a parking place. As they were hurrying toward the building, Dirk had another thought.

"Say, you weren't running quarters this morning. Not at the last."

"No, I was timing myself for tomorrow's race."

"Huh?"

"Last week I ran the mile in 4:54, which shouldn't have won me a second-place ribbon but did. Tomorrow's race will be faster. Much faster. There'll be Fisher of East and Rawlings of Lincoln. Both have done the mile in close to 4:40."

"So—?"

"So Patch can beat either, but he needs somebody to pace him."

"Why not Fisher or Rawlings? Or better yet, Patch himself?"

"I offered him my stop watch, but," Benny said ruefully, "he was afraid he'd forget to look at it. Coach Anderson won't trust Grover again. What I was doing this morning, there at the last, was timing myself for three-quarters of a mile. If I'd done it in 3:30, I'd have offered to set the pace. But I didn't come close." He shook his head. "Patch will just have to hang up close to Fisher and Rawlings."

"Nothing to worry about," Dirk said breezily. "Those boys mean business. They won't cut capers like Grover. And Patch with his finishing kick can mow them down on the homestretch."

They entered the school, and the clamor swept down upon them even as they stood in the doorway.

"That would be true and all would be simple," Benny said, "if Patch had a normal desire to win. But he just doesn't care."

"Then why should *you?*"

Benny looked at him strangely. "Maybe I shouldn't care whether Patch wins. I hadn't thought of it that way. . . . I could say, to help the school win the meet. But it's bigger than that. Call it *noblesse oblige*. The one who can do it—must! At least he must *try*."

The warning bell rang, and the boys parted to go to their lockers.

Dirk threaded his way through the halls, avoiding the crush by instinct, his thoughts on Benny. That little guy, he mused, worries too much. Worries about Patch. Patch doesn't worry at all, so he comes to the meet fresh and relaxed and ready to run.

Chapter 11

On Saturday afternoon a gusty north wind was blowing. The flag whipped out from the flagpole, and down in the lower stands a spectator's hat blew off. It skimmed away, dipped to the track, and went rolling and bouncing along on the cinders. Its owner scrambled over the rail and took off in erratic pursuit. Thirty yards down the track he pounced on his roving headgear and came trudging back, clamping the hat to his head with both hands while the crowd cheered.

Out on the field, Moose was preparing to warm up. He clenched his fists and squeezed his eyes shut. His lips started moving. Dirk stood watching, entranced.

As if feeling the stare, Moose opened his eyes and saw Dirk. "Go 'way now," Moose grunted. "I gotta talk to myself."

Dirk put his hands in his pockets and grinned. "Won't anyone else listen?"

"This is exclusive, reserved for my favorite audience."

"Well, so long, Moose. Good luck. I see that I'm needed elsewhere."

"Needed for what?" Moose scoffed.

"To hold the honey bottle for Benny."

Mr. Anderson was talking to Patch when Dirk ambled up. "That barrel-chested boy with the shock of black hair," the coach was saying, "that's Fisher. You see him, Patch?"

Patch nodded.

"The Negro boy with the long, thin legs—tallest of the three milers in purple jerseys—that's Rawlings. You see him, Patch?"

Patch nodded again.

"Stay close to those two, remember? You know the rest. Now what have I overlooked? What complications can you foresee that'll make a shambles of all our plans?"

Patch thought a moment and shook his head. "Looks like a sort of dull race comin' up, doesn't it?" he asked with a grin.

"Don't get cocky," Anderson snapped. "These boys could show you a thing or two about racing, and Fisher and Rawlings can move."

Patch's blue eyes opened wide. "I'm not overconfident, Coach. Don't think that. I—well, I just hadn't given a thought to who might win."

Five minutes later the coach was still shaking his head as he watched the runners rounding the third lap.

"No shoe-taking-off, no duck-waddles, no fifth lap—so far. Maybe our boy's beginning to grow up. He's hanging in third place like an angel."

"Or maybe a robot," Dirk murmured, "which he is not. But don't gloat too soon, Coach. The West crowd is already yelling for Patch to cut loose, and when the crowd talks, he listens."

"This time he'll listen to me. He'll wait till the last 220. He'll stay a few strides behind till he's on the backstretch in the last lap. I laid down the law."

The runners were moving toward them now down the stretch, nearing the three-quarter mark. Patch waved to them as he came down the track, still in third place. Grover was thirty yards back in fourth, and Benny was fifth, some twenty yards behind Grover. Patch passed the line and started his fourth lap.

"Cut loose, Aboriginal Jones!" the fans shouted. "Get going!"

Patch turned his head toward the crowd and listened, smiling, but he held to the same steady pace, two strides behind the leaders.

Along the outer edge of the track a girl was standing, waving her scarf at Patch as he neared. Patch smiled and waved back.

"That girl belongs in the stands," Mr. Anderson grumbled. "Must have climbed over the rail."

The blonde was waving her scarf again, and the wind was whipping the silk like a banner. Just as Patch passed her, the scarf darted out of her hand. She screamed, and the scarf took off like a live thing. It skimmed through the air, then dipped to the cinders of the outside lane and went scudding along the track like tumbleweed.

Patch broke stride. He slowed, hesitated, watching the scarf's mad progress. The girl screamed something again.

Patch glanced back over his shoulder, then angled across the empty track to the outside lane. The scarf raced along ahead of him till suddenly it dropped lifeless. Patch pounced. But the scarf was gone, dancing along ahead.

The crowd applauded and shouted encouragement. "Catch it, Patch! Catch it!"

Patch ran bent over and arms reaching, his progress as jerky as that of the scarf.

Along the inner edge of the track, Grover zipped past. A moment later Benny zipped past, calling to Patch and motioning urgently for him to get back in the race. But Patch, unhearing, was concentrating on other matters. Two more runners went by.

Zigging and zagging along the outer edge of the track, Patch spurted and slowed and pounced and missed, and spurted and slowed and dived again, while the spectators howled with delight. The last trailing runner had passed him now and had entered the curve.

With a final lunge that carried him down on one knee, Patch snatched at the elusive scarf. He leaped up and turned in triumph to face the crowd, waving the scarf in circles above his head.

The spectators cheered again, louder. The girl, still standing on the edge of the track, held out both hands for her scarf.

For the first time Patch seemed to remember that he was running a race. The girl was forty yards back now, and the runners were far ahead. He glanced at the scarf as if wondering what to do with it, now that he finally had it. He reached behind him and stuffed one end of it into the waistband of his trunks. Then he whirled and took out after the others, head down and legs churning like a sprinter's.

"Come on, Patch!" Dirk shouted between cupped hands.

Mr. Anderson stared at him bleakly. "Why not yell for somebody who deserves it?"

Dirk glanced at the coach's grim face and followed his eyes across the field. The runners were strung out along the backstretch, but where three men had been running well in the lead there were now only two. The Lincoln boy's long brown legs were pumping as smoothly as pistons, eating up yardage. Two strides behind him the barrel-chester Fisher was pounding along. Both were about to enter the curve.

Forty yards back was Grover, in third place. Fifteen yards behind him came Benny. And far at the other end of the backstretch was Patch.

"He lost more than a hundred yards!" wailed Dirk.

The crowd was still chanting for Patch, laughing and pointing and cheering him on. Patch was running with joyous abandon, free to cut loose, and he did. He roared down the track. The scarf, tucked into his waistband, soared straight out behind him and flapped in the wind like a tail.

"Heigh-ho, Silver!" somebody bellowed.

Patch heard him somehow and tossed his head and kept running. He overtook the last man, and the spectators shouted again.

"You think he can make up the distance?" Dirk asked eagerly.

Mr. Anderson shook his head. "And maybe that's good," he added.

At the north end of the grandstand a shout arose. All heads turned to see Rawlings and Fisher battling it out in the stretch. In that instant Patch was forgotten. Fisher, in the final sprint for the tape, edged closer until his left shoulder was almost touching Rawlings. But Rawlings of Lincoln called forth one last effort and flung himself gasping into the tape while the crowd screamed.

Now the heads turned again to the start of the home-stretch. Benny was swinging wide to pass Grover. Grover glanced over his shoulder and quickened his pace. The spectators started shouting once more.

Watching them driving toward him, Dirk knew that both runners were spent. Grover was beginning to weave, and Benny's shoulders were hunched with fatigue. Behind him a boy in a purple jersey was drawing closer.

Grover eyed the finish line longingly, and each time his front foot stabbed the cinders his head wobbled a bit. Behind him, Benny was inching closer, his face drawn and his shoulders hunched even more. Now the boy in the purple jersey was pounding dangerously close behind. The crowd was on its feet, screaming.

Five yards from the finish line Benny gathered his strength for a final burst. As he moved up to pass, Grover lurched to the right. Benny swung wide to avoid a collision. In that split second the boy in the purple jersey slipped past on the inside, where Grover had vacated the pole. The stranger swept across the finish line to garner third-place honors a whisker ahead of Grover and Benny.

Now Patch came romping along the stretch, the scarf still fluttering tail-like behind. A ripple of laughter ran through the crowd, but no cheers followed. Patch threw back his head and neighed like a horse.

Coach Anderson muttered something between his teeth. To Dirk it sounded suspiciously like "bray of a jackass."

"Heigh-ho, Silverware," somebody called.

"Look at the horse's tail," somebody answered, and a snicker rippled across the crowd.

Patch crossed the line with a faraway look in his eyes, as if searching for someone. Dirk could guess who she was. He turned, expecting to see her still standing beside the track, her hands reaching out for the scarf. But she had vanished.

An hour later the team trudged wearily into the dressing room and flung themselves onto the benches.

A curly-haired boy put his head in his hands. "To lose the relay by inches!" he said, still short of breath and half-choking. "Inches! I thought I had him at the tape. I thought I'd caught him. But there was the tape snapping in front of me—and I wasn't quite there yet. I don't see yet how it happened. And then to lose the whole meet by just those few points—those few inches!"

"My fault," a boy said gruffly, stooping to untie his shoes. He straightened up. "If I hadn't lost several yards in the third leg, you'd have gotten an even start, Curly, and then we'd have won."

"But to lose the meet by so little—"

"You guys," Dirk said, "ran the fastest relay you've ever run. Passed the baton real slick and beat out one team supposed to be faster than you and almost beat out another."

"You did swell," the high jumper said. "It was my fault we lost. I've cleared two inches higher than I jumped today. If I'd done it today, I'd have had a first instead of a tie for second." He shook his head. "Just didn't seem to have the lift. I could feel it in the take-off toward the last. Kind of a dead feeling in my legs."

"It was my fault we lost," said Bill Adams, the dashman. "I figured to win the hundred, but I got away slow and couldn't catch up. I'll have to work on my start."

Patch sat quietly, fingering the fresh gauze square on his knee, the knee he had scraped on the cinders in retrieving the scarf.

"How's your knee, Patch?" Sax asked.

"Oh, it's nothing."

All eyes turned to Patch's knee and next to the scarf that lay in a heap on his lap. Sudden stillness filled the room. Patch looked around at two dozen pairs of eyes, all staring at him.

"I—I guess it was my fault we lost the meet." He sounded surprised. No one denied his statement. Nobody said a word. The silence resumed.

"Maybe I shouldn't have gone after that scarf," Patch said, musing. "She seemed sort of—helpless—and I was right there—" He hesitated. "Not that I'm Sir Walter Raleigh. It was sort of a game—a challenge—"

The silence continued.

"Well, I'm sorry I lost us the meet," Patch said.

The team sat in stony-faced silence. Coach Anderson was leaning against the wall, hands in his pockets. A ghost of a smile was playing around his mouth.

"Well," Patch repeated, "I'm sorry if I lost us the meet. I'm sorry I chased the scarf—I guess. . . . But it sure was fun while it lasted!" He smiled to himself, remembering. "The crowd got a bang out of it too, didn't they?" He looked around, grinning hopefully.

The same stony faces stared back.

"Next week," said Moose, "they'll be rolling apples down the track for you to chase."

"And the week after that they'll start tossing you peanuts."

Patch looked around from one angry face to another, his own face blank with amazement.

"Don't look now," Sax put in, "but your show is slipping."

Coach Anderson peeled himself off the wall. "Okay, fellows," he said, stepping into the middle of the room. "This was a tough one to lose, but next Friday we'll face these same teams again in the city meet. We can make up for it then. To the showers now."

The boys rose slowly, stretching, talking, grumbling. One or two of them glared at Patch.

"Patch and Grover, wait up!" Mr. Anderson said.

When the others had gone to the showers, Mr. Anderson spoke. "Simply a matter of convenience," he said in a disarmingly soft voice. "You have a scarf, Patch."

He nodded toward the scarf now trailing from Patch's hand. "You'd like to see that it gets to its rightful owner?"

"Yes! She—"

"Give it to Grover."

Patch raised his hand reluctantly. "Why?"

"He'll see that she gets it. You see, Patch—" The coach turned, and his eyes bored into Grover. "By the merest coincidence, your lady and Grover go steady."

Chapter 12

Monday afternoon Dirk trudged with lagging steps down the stadium stairs to the fieldhouse. Somehow the thought of practice bored him today. In half an hour the team would report, and they would be even wearier than he after Saturday's meet.

He entered the fieldhouse and stopped at the door of the coach's office. "Any special instructions today, Mr. A.? You want all the equipment out?"

"Why, no." Mr. A. laid down his pencil and raised his head. "Here, I was just going to post this." He held out a slip of paper.

Dirk read it and leaped into the air, clicking his heels. "No practice today! Oh boy oh boy oh boy oh. . . . How come?"

Mr. Anderson took the slip and strolled out to the bulletin board. "I figure we're in for a sort of letdown," he said, driving a thumbtack in with his huge thumb. "The quickest way to get past it is just to go off and forget about track. One practice session won't make or break us, and a bit of relaxation will help the boys get in shape mentally for the heavy end of the schedule now coming up."

"Psychology, hey? The Casey Stengel of the Cinders." Mr. Anderson quirked an eyebrow.

"Since there's no equipment to set up, Coach, then—uh—I should go back to study hall for the rest of the period?" Dirk asked, hoping that he sounded as reluctant as he felt.

The coach sat down on the edge of the table and swung his legs. "Yes indeed—if you have lessons to get. But if you'd only sit in study hall and twiddle your thumbs, you can do that here while a grizzled old coach goes into the matter of the so-called adolescent mind."

Dirk flopped happily on a bench and drew up his feet.

"I need a sounding board," the coach went on. "A sound adolescent one. Someone I can talk to in the full confidence that what I say stops with *him*."

Dirk nodded, flattered. He noted that Mr. Anderson was in one of his rare moods of garrulity, and there were many things Dirk wanted to know. On one point, in fact, he couldn't restrain himself.

"That girl with the scarf," he said, "I'd never seen her before. How did you know she's Grover's steady?"

"Elementary," said Mr. Anderson. "You don't know her because she goes to East High. I live on the East Side myself, and I've seen them together in movies and eating places." He added, "Of course, I don't really know how exclusive their arrangement is."

"I get you," Dirk said. "Grover would hate to deprive some other pretty girl of his company when his kitten's clear across town." He stopped as another thought struck him. "Hey! You don't think Grover had anything to do with—"

"All I know is what my five senses tell me. I saw Grover leaning over the rail talking to her during the meet. Innocent enough in itself."

Dirk thought a moment. "*After* the fat man's hat blew off?"

The coach nodded. "After."

"Mmm! You suspect—?"

Mr. Anderson shrugged. "What I suspect and what I can prove are two different things. In fact, that seems to be the pattern. Take Saturday's race. Did Grover weave over in front of Benny, there at the last, to prevent Benny from passing? Or was it purely an accident? It might well have been. Grover was weaving from weariness anyhow and should have got off the track— except that he was so close to the finish line, and you can't blame a boy for trying to finish. Especially when three more steps might bring him a ribbon."

"Yeah. So neither of 'em got the ribbon."

"Take the week before, when he set that ridiculously fast pace and had to drop out. I don't believe for a minute that he thought he was running the 880. And yet . . . he had a second-place ribbon cinched, and he knew it. Does one boy ever resent another so much that he tosses away a second-place ribbon just to prevent the other from winning a first?"

"If he did, he didn't," Dirk said. "Didn't prevent it, I mean."

"And there's still the strange case of the shoes. As Patch says, all I know is that first they were there, and then they weren't, and then they were there again. Grover had the motive. Grover had the opportunity. And yet—who is the only person who verifies that Patch remembered to pack his shoes?"

"Grover."

"Maybe Grover's a sly one. If he is . . . that kind, you just have to give them enough rope. I intend to. . . . On the other hand—and this is the only part that you should remember—every man must be assumed innocent until he is proved guilty."

"Aw, I think you're too easy on him, Coach, considering—"

"I'm not a soft man, Dirk. But I'd rather be duped three times over than run the chance of marking a boy for life by accusing him when he's innocent."

Dirk nodded.

"Now, getting back to the runaway scarf and the girl friend," Mr. Anderson said. "Does Patch suspect that maybe she didn't *try* to hold on to the scarf? Does he suspect that Grover's fine hand might have written the script and directed the scene?"

"Patch? Why, he's such a sweet little guy, he wouldn't suspect a man who walked in with a handkerchief over his face and a bulge in his pocket."

Anderson smiled. "That's good."

"It is? Why?"

"I'd been sitting there at my desk," the coach said, "trying to figure. What happens to a fun-loving kid's love of fun once he gets suckered? Once his wonderful nonsense is turned back upon him like a gun?"

"Now slow down, Coach. I'm not sure I follow. You mean you want Patch to stay as he is? You mean you want him to keep doing zany things?"

"Maybe I want too much, Dirk." Mr. Anderson cupped his chin thoughtfully. "I want him to stay as he is, and I want him to change completely. I might even say, *I* want to change him—largely by staying behind the scenes and pulling the right strings."

"And which are the right strings?"

"I sure wish I knew." Mr. Anderson shook his head. "But you're one of them. Benny's another."

Dirk straightened up. "What do you want us to do?"

"Right now, just listen. Just listen while I mull this over, and later you can drop a word now and then at the right moment to Patch. You see, Dirk," he said, leaning forward earnestly, "I believe that a coach must do more than just train a boy to run a mile in 4:40 or high jump six feet. He must teach the boy to master his personality."

"I'm—uh—not sure what that last part means."

The coach chuckled. "Neither am I," he murmured. "We educators love our words and our phrases. But in Patch's case I mean this. First of all, he's a boy who dearly loves to run—the greatest asset a runner could have. In his love of his sport he's like Willie Mays, the ball player. Came time one spring for Willie to sign a new contract. Did Willie haggle about his salary? He didn't even ask how much it would be—just picked up the pen and signed. 'Only thing I care about is playing ball,' Willie said, and anyone who watches him play can see how he loves it. That spirit earned him the title of

101

Most Valuable Player of the National League. It can do wonderful things for Patch too, if nobody tampers with it. Last thing I'd want to do would be stifle it."

Dirk nodded.

"Another thing I don't want to change," the coach continued, "is this. He's a fun-loving kid. That inward amusement will serve as an armor all through life. I'd be taking more than I gave if I took it away. That's why—in case you wondered—I haven't chewed him out for Saturday's wild performance."

"Yeah, I sure did wonder."

"On the other hand, he'll have to learn to master it and turn it to useful purposes, even if it's nothing more than laughing over spilt milk."

"And yet," Dirk mused, "you leaned there against the wall and let the team chew him out. Most of the time, of course, nobody said a word—and yet they were saying plenty by keeping quiet."

The grizzled head bobbed. "Wonderful job those boys did. I stopped them after they'd made their point and before they belabored it. In fact, they made two points. They taught Patch to think of himself as part of a *team* for the first time. He has more to learn about teamwork, of course, but this was a start. Also, they cured an incipient case of grandstanditis."

"Of which?"

"Playing to the grandstand. I got goose flesh Saturday, Dirk, watching him practically bow to the crowd. Many a good athlete has had his head turned by a few cheers."

102

"Oh, yes, he's told me about the cheers. He said he came here from Millville, and for three days he walked through the halls of the biggest building he'd ever been in, meaning West. He said he passed thousands of students—though we know, of course, that there aren't more than sixteen hundred—and nobody spoke. Not one person. Then at the interclass track meet and tryouts, all of a sudden hundreds of kids were yelling his name. After the tryouts, when he went back into the building, a dozen people or more called him 'Patch' as they passed in the hall."

Anderson nodded. "That was the start."

"After the first local meet," Dirk went on, "more people knew him and spoke. And when Sax's column came out, everyone called him 'Aboriginal Jones.' Everyone spoke. He loved it."

"Sure," Mr. Anderson murmured. "Print anything at all about me, just so you put it on the front page." He hesitated. "That isn't true of Patch though. He's not a publicity hound. And he isn't really a grandstander. Pray that he never will be. To avoid it, he'll need to learn three things."

"What?"

"First, team spirit. There isn't much teamwork in track, to be sure. It's an individual sport. But there's always the thought of the team victory. Not that it ever occurred to Patch before Saturday, down in that dressing room.

"Secondly," he continued, "a sense of responsibility, which is part of the painful process of growing up. In his case it means a job to do and he does it."

103

"Benny called it *noblesse oblige*," Dirk put in. "The one who can do it, he says, *must*."

"That's right. There's another thing that Benny knows too and Patch needs to learn. Concentration. He should be so intent on what goes on in the race that he isn't even aware that a crowd is watching."

"That's a big order—for Patch," Dirk said. "Those bright eyes dart everywhere, and he hears—I'd swear—with every inch of his body."

"A big order," the coach agreed, nodding, "and there's one that's bigger. Competitive spirit!"

"You know, Mr. Anderson, I don't think Patch really cares whether he wins or not. And now I'm all mixed up. I've read so many articles that say there's too much emphasis on winning—too much concern with success. Whether you win or not doesn't matter, the articles say. . . . And yet—when you actually *see* a fellow who doesn't half try to win, you wonder. Me, I'll take the guy who knocks himself out trying."

Anderson slammed the table with the flat of his hand. The sound shot through the room like the crack of a rifle, and Dirk jumped.

"Don't *ever*," the coach said, thrusting out his jaw, "don't ever get confused about that. Yes, there's too much emphasis on winning—when it means cheating to win; when it means heavy subsidies to college players; when it means firing the coach who has done a good job. *But*—what I'm talking about is a personal matter. Strictly between a boy and himself."

He leaned forward. "Get this, Dirk! I'd like to shout it to high school students from sea to sea. I'd like to write

104

it in letters as high as the sky." His voice seemed to vibrate with intensity. "Don't *ever* be ashamed that you yearn to win! The desire to win is as essential in life as in sport. It demands of a man that he do his level best. It calls forth the all-out effort. It makes for perfection, achievement, precision workmanship. It makes, in short, the leader—the *un*common man, and that's the man we're all looking for, despite our lip service to the common man and our gutless glorification of mediocrity."

Relaxing, he leaned back and cradled his knee. "I remember a story," he mused, "that my sportswriter friend Dan Scism once told. One night after a college basketball game the coach and some friends had gone to a restaurant. They were sitting around, eating and talking, when the college coach asked, 'Did you see what that freshman from Mackey did when he sank that winning goal? He pounded his chest with both fists and roared like Tarzan. I love that kid! I've got me an All-American there.' "

"Did the player make All-American?"

"He did." The coach shifted his position and leaned back on one hand. "Offhand," he continued, "I can't think of a single great athlete who lacked a fierce—a burning—desire to win. Ask any major-league baseball scout what he looks for. He'll tell you—natural ability *plus* competitive spirit. Without it, many an athlete with worlds of talent has faded away, unheard of, all his ability wasted."

"You think," Dirk asked hesitantly, "you think that might happen to Patch?"

"I think it might and it will—unless we do something

about it! You know"—he spoke softly now—"a high school coach doesn't get many chances like this. Twenty-five years I've been coaching, and this is the first time I really could say that one of my boys is marked for greatness. . . . *If!* . . ."

Dirk was silent, awed. A moment later his roseate dreams were shattered by the clang of the school bell.

Chapter 13

As the echo of the bell died away, Mr. Anderson slid off the table and pivoted toward his office. "Well, school's out. In half a minute the thundering herd will descend on us. I'll be in here in case anyone wants to see me. You might hang around a few minutes, Dirk, to make sure that everyone sees the notice."

"Check," Dirk said and posted himself at the door.

The first arrival was Benny. He read the notice solemnly, nodded approval, and walked to his locker and unlocked it.

"Hey!" Dirk protested. "You don't have to dress today. No practice."

Benny looked up and smiled. "I thought I might take this chance to file the spikes of my track shoes, yes?"

Thereafter each time somebody entered, Dirk jerked his thumb toward the bulletin board, then listened with satisfaction to the exclamations of pleasure. Soon the locker room was agog with a babble of voices.

"Two wonderful big fat hours to kill," Moose rumbled. "Nothin' to do—except go home and help with the spring house cleaning!"

By two's and three's the boys straggled out. All but a few had departed when Patch appeared.

"Number 28. That means last," Dirk said with a snort as he jerked his thumb.

Patch read the notice and grinned. "Too bad," he murmured. "No practice. I wanted to brush up on catching peanuts."

"You're lucky you're not catching you-know-what," Dirk answered. He looked around. Benny was filing his spikes. Moose was lolling on the bench, apparently in no great hurry to dash home to help with the house cleaning. The others had left.

"Why don't we all go down to the drugstore?" Dirk suggested.

Moose lumbered to his feet. "Dirk, that idea makes you a whiz-kid."

Benny looked up from his filing. "What will we do at the drugstore?"

"Who cares?" Moose asked.

"Oh, just eat and talk awhile," Dirk said.

"Certainly I'd enjoy it, but there's the matter of eating between meals. Mr. Anderson told us—"

"Aw, Benny," Patch protested, "today's a holiday. No practice." He turned to Dirk. "Where's the drugstore?"

"West Side Drug. Seven or eight blocks. I'll take you all in my car."

"Not me. I've been sitting all day. Meet you there."

"Okay, Aboriginal, you run," Moose said, stretching. "Me, I'll ride with Dirk."

"We'll get a booth and order for you," Dirk told Patch. "What do you want?"

"Chocolate ice cream."

"The same for me," Benny said, putting his track shoes back in his locker. "I'll go with Patch. I know the way."

A few minutes later Dirk was backing into a parking place near the drugstore. As he and Moose walked to the door, Dirk looked far up the street. "I don't see Patch and Benny yet, but they ought to be here pretty soon."

"They are," Moose said as he opened the door to the drugstore. Dirk looked over Moose's shoulder. In the first booth, grinning proudly, sat the two milers.

"Poor service here," Patch commented when Dirk and Moose joined them. "We thought we'd order for you and have your ice cream half eaten before you'd walked that block to your car."

"Judging from the huffing and puffing I hear," Dirk observed, "the ice cream wouldn't have started to melt yet even if you'd scooped it up as you passed the counter."

"Benny," said Patch, "it hurts him to think we outran his jalopy."

"Even Grover can outrun that thing," Moose scoffed.

"And outrun me too," Benny added ruefully.

"Well now, I'm not so sure," Moose said. "Looked to me Saturday as if you were on your way past him when he veered over into your path."

Benny shrugged. "I can't really blame him for that. I made some mistakes of my own. I violated one of Norris McWhirter's two laws of acceleration."

"Never heard of McWhirter or his laws," Patch said.

"Oh, yes. You heard about one of them from Grover

before the first regular meet, though I doubt that he knew the source. *He who accelerates from behind wins.*"

"Yeah, the pacemaker rhubarb."

"The other is *He who accelerates twice is lost.* I tried accelerating twice—and lost."

"Well," Patch said blandly, "I wouldn't lose any sleep over it. There's no disgrace in losing."

"That depends," Benny answered, leaning forward on the table thoughtfully. "The only disgrace lies in losing by such things as laziness—or cowardice—or stupidity—or—"

"Or chasing a scarf?" Moose asked softly.

At that moment the waitress appeared with their ice cream, which turned out to be vanilla. Moose leaned over and looked down into his dish.

"A moth ball!" he snorted.

"This business of winning or losing," Benny hurried on, "reminds me of something I read. It's what Roger Bannister said at a big dinner being held in his honor. He'd run the first four-minute mile in history that year, '54, and he got up to make a speech. He told them that he was going to take a hospital appointment. He's a doctor, you know? And then he announced out of the blue that he was going to give up running. 'I shall not have sufficient time to put up a first-class performance,' Bannister told his shocked audience. 'There would be little satisfaction for me in a second-rate performance,' Bannister explained, 'and it would be wrong for me to give one when representing my country.'"

Patch stopped with his spoon poised halfway to his

110

mouth. "Wrong to run a four-minute mile—or close to it?"

"Wrong to do less than his best!" Benny answered.

"Mmm." Patch didn't sound convinced.

"I suppose," Benny added, "you've read what he said when somebody asked him how he could run a four-minute mile, no?"

Patch shook his head.

"Bannister said, 'It's the ability to take more out of yourself than you've got.'"

Patch shook his head again, dubiously this time. "How can you take more out than is there?"

"I'll give you a minor example," Benny answered. "Take Saturday."

"Not Saturday," Patch murmured, pushing it away with his hand. "I'm giving that back to the Indians."

"Take Saturday," Benny went on, ignoring him. "I ran the fastest mile I've ever run in my life. As I came down the homestretch, the finish line seemed to get farther and farther away. The last twenty yards seemed to last forever. My legs just kept moving automatically—there was nothing left to make them move. But when I was about five yards from the finish, I saw that if I could get up just one burst of speed I could pass Grover. And the energy came from somewhere."

"You sure were a tired little boy at the finish," Dirk said.

"I want it that way. An American Olympic coach once said that if you can run another step past the tape, you'll know that you didn't try as hard as you could've."

111

Dirk looked at Patch, who had laid down his spoon to listen. Now Patch picked up his spoon and started to eat again, glassy-eyed, as if he were grappling with a new idea. The foursome ate in silence.

The door creaked, and Moose looked around. "Oh-oh. Don't look now but here come Grover and Sax with two babes."

The couples swept past, Grover with a black-haired minx and Sax with a redhead. They sat down in the booth just behind the four boys.

"That was that cute Patch Jones," a girl's voice said with a titter. "I thought he was a riot Saturday."

Dirk noted with disapproval that Patch had come out of his trance and was beaming with pleasure.

"That cute Patch Jones," Grover muttered in a voice pitched to carry into the next booth, "has been reading Dizzy Dean."

"Or trying to emulate him," Sax's voice said.

"Reading him, Sax," Grover corrected silkily. "Reading an article Diz once wrote, in which he started out by saying that in his home town in Arkansas there were two barbers, Emory and Fillmore. Fillmore says to Diz one day, 'Jay Hanna, whyn't anybody ever come to *my* shop?' So Diz tells him. Emory could play a tune with his scissors. Emory could make his beard stand at half-mast. 'Well,' Diz says, 'Fillmore catched on fast.' He had a dentist put two diamonds in his front teeth, and he learned to wiggle his ears. And then both barbers got rich."

"Will Patch get rich?" the girl asked.

"Nobody gets rich in track, wool-head," Sax snapped. "Not even Wes Santee."

"Well, anyhow, Sax, I think you ought to put that in your column."

"My column's already written."

Grover's voice came again, louder. "I really don't recommend diamonds. They wouldn't show at a distance. But Patch could get his reading friend Benny to tell him about Wilt the Stilt Chamberlain."

"What about Wilt?" Sax prodded.

"In track meets Wilt wears a plaid cap that he never takes off, even when high jumping."

"Patch does better than that," the girl said. "*He* wears a tail."

"Why don't you put *that* in your column, Sax?" the other girl asked.

"I told you my column's already written."

"Well, what did you say about Patch?"

Dirk and his friends heard a great sigh and then the rattle of paper. "Here," Sax said. "That's the first draft, the longhand copy of what I wrote about Patch."

"Read it aloud, Nancy," the other said.

"No!" This was Sax's voice.

But Nancy was already reading.

West High thinlies lost a heartbreaker Saturday. One more blue ribbon would have won us the meet. Track being ordinarily the most predictable of sports, the consensus around the locker room was that our chances went down the drain when a cer-

tain applause-meter reader chose to make like a
horse. As a result, what this miler garnered in points
was a horse collar. And there went the meet. To top
off the floperoo, he didn't look like a horse, after all.
Only one part of a horse.

"One part of a horse? Which part? . . . Oh! . . .
Why, Sax, I think you're mean!" Nancy said. "I thought
he was cute. Track needs more color, and Patch was only
being a gentleman." There was a pause, and the same
voice continued, "But if he really lost us the meet, that's
different. . . . I *hate* a grandstander!"

"Here, let me see the article," the other girl said.

Another pause followed, and then the girl's voice came
again. "How come this is *your* handwriting, Grover?"

Chapter 14

Grover finished a practice lap Wednesday afternoon and pulled up.

"Coach, did you take my time on that lap?" he called.

"No, but you sure did," Mr. Anderson rumbled.

Twenty feet away Sax Warner doubled over in silent laughter. Grover turned slowly, and Sax straightened up, turned away, and tried to pucker his lips in an unconcerned whistle.

"Patch!" Mr. Anderson called, and Patch came trotting over. "Let's see you do a quarter in seventy-one," the coach said. "Use that stop watch you bought yourself Monday afternoon. Let's see if you've got the hang of it yet. Start here and I'll check your time."

Patch stood at the starting line and fiddled with his stop watch. "Ready?" he asked.

Mr. Anderson nodded, and Patch took off with a crunching of cinders. Dirk strolled over beside the coach to observe. Patch was already approaching the curve. He whirled around it without consulting the watch.

"Too fast, too fast." The coach stood shaking his head.

115

"Some day—if I live that long—I'll get me a boy who knows when he's running fast—and can."

"He hasn't even glanced at the stop watch," Dirk grumbled.

Now Patch was sailing along the backstretch. As he approached the midway mark, he suddenly remembered the watch. From across the field Dirk and the coach saw Patch's hand come up and his head jerk down. He stared at the watch, shook it briefly, and held it against his ear. Apparently it was still running. Patch slowed at once, stopped, and sat down on the track. He sat there crosslegged for several seconds. Then he leaped to his feet and bounded away.

Rounding the curve, he consulted the watch again. All the way down the homestretch he checked it at every step. As he crossed the finish line where Dirk and the coach were standing he called back over his shoulder triumphantly, "I did it! Seventy-one on the nose."

Mr. Anderson clicked off his own watch. "How true," he murmured, "how true. . . . What do you do with a boy like that?"

An hour later the coach called the milers around him. "Well, now about Friday's meet," he said. "The city meet. This is the first of our three major meets, and the only one of the three to be held in Crescent City. The city meet is big—big in importance and big in the number of entries."

Grover beamed with pride.

"How big?" Patch asked. "How many high schools in Crescent City?"

"Seven," Mr. Anderson said, "and they'll all be competing in this one. I doubt that all seven will enter three men in the mile, but you can count on a big field—and no sections, only the one race. That means you'll have to avoid getting boxed. If you run directly behind the man ahead and someone comes up alongside you, brother, you're boxed."

"Boxing," Benny pointed out, "is illegal."

"So it is, but officials tend to be lenient because often a box is unintentional. Avoid it by staying to the right of the runner ahead of you—off his right shoulder. You can get out of a box by slowing down and running around the man on the outside. But it costs you a few yards, and yards mean seconds."

All three boys nodded in understanding.

"About our plan for the race," the coach continued. "Last year Grover won this one—"

Grover nodded and smiled modestly.

"—in a time of 4:47," Mr. Anderson said. "That won't win it this year. Those two boys you faced last week— Rawlings and Fisher—are vastly improved this season. Their time last week was 4:42. There's a miler at Cathedral who's done 4:44. Those three are the ones to watch.

"Thanks to certain shenanigans which *will not be repeated*," he went on, "we're in a position to pull a sleeper."

"What do you mean, sir?" Benny asked.

"Patch didn't show his speed last Saturday. He might surprise Rawlings and Fisher. And somehow, in the general confusion of the mile run in our first triangular meet, the official timekeeper failed to get Patch's time, possi-

117

bly because the tape wasn't out. Upstate, in the indoor meet, nobody bothered to clock him because of his late start. So he's truly a dark horse, and some people around town are in for a big surprise."

"I'm afraid, sir," Benny said, shaking his head, "it's you. Have you seen this morning's paper?"

"No. Haven't had time. Why?"

"There's an article in it about Patch. I read it in the school library this morning."

"Dirk," the coach snapped, "streak up to the library and ask to borrow today's paper. Hurry!"

In a few minutes Dirk was back, winded, with the Crescent City *Star* clutched under his arm.

Benny spread the paper on the grass, turned quickly to the right page, and jabbed a thin forefinger at the sports editor's column. "This paragraph."

The three milers, Mr. Anderson, and Dirk all knelt on the grass to read.

Among the standouts in tomorrow's city track meet will be Jim Perkins, East's topflight pole vaulter; Moose Elliot, the man-mountain shot-putter from West; and Lincoln's lean and limber timber-topper, Lawson Larrimore. An enigma who has yet to run his best race—and might do it Friday evening —is junior Patch Jones of West.

The unpredictable Jones showed flashes of greatness last Saturday, and we don't mean by catching the scarf. While the spectators were watching Rawlings and Fisher battle it out in the stretch, Jones was scorching the track unnoticed. In less than a lap he made up a cool forty yards of the hundred he'd frittered away, and this without seeming to extend himself fully. Our nomination for dark-horse winner of the longest run of the day tomorrow: Patch Jones.

Coach Anderson pushed himself up slowly. "Well . . . this changes my plans."

"What were they?" Grover asked.

"Same as last week, Patch to lay behind Rawlings and Fisher and then cut loose with a finishing kick, which neither of them seems to have."

Grover shrugged. "Why change? But of course, our boy owns a stop watch now. He can set his own pace."

Mr. Anderson shook his head. "Too early. Too risky. He might not remember to look."

Patch grinned ruefully. "I'll try! . . . But I can't be sure. When I get on a track in these featherweight shoes, and the spikes sort of pull me along, I want to go faster and faster. . . . Maybe I'd just better do what you said, lay behind Rawlings and Fisher."

Mr. Anderson gnawed at his lower lip.

"No, the coach was right," Benny put in, "when he said that this article changes his plans. Rawlings and Fisher, knowing that they don't finish fast and Patch can, will have a defense worked out."

"Such as?" Grover scoffed.

"Such as the one John Landy devised."

"Oh? Something you've read no doubt?"

Benny nodded. "You might call John Landy the virtuoso of track. After his loss to Roger Bannister in the Mile of the Century, Landy became discouraged. He didn't see

119

how the man who sets the pace—which Landy does—ever could win a close race. The only alternative seemed to be to follow, however slow the pace. But Landy said, 'I'd rather lose a 3:58 mile than win one in 4:10.' "

"Not me!" Grover muttered.

"Then," Benny continued, "Landy conceived the idea that the hunted, as he calls the pacers, could discourage the hunters by setting an uneven pace—specifically by speeding up and pulling beyond striking distance just where the hunters like to slow down to gather their strength—on the third lap."

Grover the hunted looked thoughtful.

"What if Fisher or Rawlings try that?" Patch asked. "Or what if only one of them does? Which one will I follow?"

Mr. Anderson hesitated.

"You want me to set the pace?" Grover asked.

"Thanks, I think not," the coach answered.

"That doesn't leave anyone," Benny said, "but me. What pace would you like?"

"I'd like to see Patch break the city record of 4:37.6!"

Benny lifted his thin shoulders and spread his hands. "Patch has run much faster than that when it didn't count," Mr. Anderson said. "But this time he'd have to do most of it on his own. And he might run himself right out of the race in the first two laps."

Patch flushed and looked down at his shiny new stop watch. He dug up a bit of turf with the spikes of one shoe but said nothing. A moment of silence followed.

Mr. Anderson sighed. "The record was set two years

ago, and that fellow's long gone," he continued after the pause. "I think a 4:40 would win it this year."

"It just so happens," Benny suggested hesitantly, "that I've been practicing running quarters in seventy seconds flat. Usually they turn out to be seventy-one though. And I've never been able yet to put four seventy-ones together. But I'm reasonably certain that I can do three laps in seventy-one seconds each. Would that help?"

The drawn look vanished from Mr. Anderson's face. He jerked a pad and a stub of pencil out of his pocket and began to figure rapidly.

"Fisher and Rawlings are fairly consistent runners. If they turn in another 4:42 and Benny runs on the basis of a 4:44 mile, then at the end of three laps Patch at Benny's shoulder will be only about ten yards behind the leaders."

"In that case," asked Grover, "why bother? Why not just let Rawlings and Fisher set the pace for Patch?"

"We've already gone into that. This is on the basis of over-all performance and eliminates the possibility of Patch being led astray by changes in pace such as Benny mentioned."

"What do I do at the end of three quarters?" Patch asked.

"Maintain the same pace until you see the right time to speed up and pass. Give it a burst of speed when you know you can hold the faster pace all the way to the finish. That lap you'll have to do on your own."

Patch nodded. A second later a frown swept his face. "How about Benny?"

"What I do after the first three quarters won't matter," Benny said quickly.

"Sure it will. Maybe you won't be able to finish—"

"It won't matter. Look at it this way, Patch. At least four men in this race are faster than I."

"But in the city meet," Patch protested, "the first *five* finishers win ribbons and points."

"What we need is a first," Benny answered, "not a fifth."

"Well—I don't like it . . ."

"We're all set for Friday, Patch, thanks to Benny," Mr. Anderson said. "If you don't like the arrangements, you're the one—and the only one—who can see that they won't be necessary again. You can go to the showers now, all three of you."

They straggled across the field, Benny and Grover together and Patch with Dirk. Patch was silent, fingering his new stop watch.

"That Benny," he said after a while. "I can just tell by looking how bad he wants to win, and now he won't have a chance. He'll have to run himself out too early."

Dirk did not answer, and Patch continued to plod along, studying the stop watch absently. As he turned to go into the locker room Patch said, "I guess I won't be riding home with you after practice today, Dirk. Not today nor probably all next week."

"Why not?"

"Oh—just say I'm a kid with a new toy. There are a lot of quarters to time between here and home."

Dirk's face lit up. "Maybe you'll make a miler yet,

Aboriginal." He stopped. "But how will you know when you've run exactly four hundred and forty yards?"

Patch looked blank. "Hadn't thought about that."

"Tell you what, Patch. Ride home with me this afternoon and we'll clock it on the speedometer. We'll pick up a landmark every time two and a half tenths turn up. I'll take you all the way home. We'll make a list of the landmarks. You can start running it next week."

"Yippee!" Patch yiped. He leaped up and grabbed the top edge of the locker-room door and dangled there for a moment by one arm, scratching his chest with the other hand like a monkey and uttering simian sounds of delight.

Chapter 15

The slanting sunlight angled down on the bright green grass. It was the dinner hour, but no one gave it a thought. The air was crackling with excitement, and the grandstand at East High was crammed to its farthest reaches for the first and only time till the football season next fall.

Dirk watched the mob of milers milling around at the starting line. Suddenly Benny darted out of the group and grabbed Dirk's arm.

"Where's Mr. Anderson?"

"Across the field, giving somebody some last-minute advice. This is a three-ring circus. Why? You milers are all set, aren't you?"

"We were, but now I'm worried. That crowd! If Patch is loose for a full lap in front of a crowd so large, what will he do? I believe I might be able to hold that seventy-one-second pace for another half lap. Do you think I should try? Do you think Patch should stay behind me that long?"

Dirk wished mightily for Mr. Anderson. "Well . . ." he said, pondering. "The coach always says, if you think you're outmanned, gamble. If you think you can win, play it safe. I think we can win, and having Patch stick with you another half lap would be playing it safe. Or would it? Let's see how far behind you'd be at the end of three and a half laps. . . ."

He bent his head over his clipboard and figured quickly. "Ten yards divided by. . . . Why, you'd only lose another yard and a half! Patch would have eleven and a half yards to make up instead of ten. He can do that."

Benny beamed. "I'm not positive I can hold the pace that long, you understand. Patch should pass me as soon as he sees me begin to weaken."

Dirk nodded. "Send him over here and I'll tell him."

Benny scampered back into the group, and a second later Patch emerged.

"What's up?" he asked.

Dirk explained the extended plan.

As Patch listened a frown creased his forehead. "I'd been kinda hoping," he said when Dirk finished, "that maybe I could get the coach his new record after all. Maybe I could. We'll do the first three quarters in 3:33, and then I cut loose. The city record is 4:37.6, he said. If I could do the last lap in sixty-four and a half—"

"Do you think you could—after three fairly fast laps?"

"Gosh, I don't know. . . . I don't really know *what* I can do. . . . Should I try?"

Dirk groaned. "Only Mr. Anderson could answer that one." He gazed longingly across the field. . . . "Look, he's starting this way! Holy mother-of-pearl, if he'd only hurry!"

125

As they watched, the coach was walking briskly toward them across the field. "I know how much he wants you to set a new record," Dirk said. "But we can't take a wild chance on our own. We need a first in this race. If not a first, then we've *got* to have a second."

From out of the milling mob of milers came Grover's voice calling. "Has Benny had his snort yet? Then let the race begin."

The runners were moving into their lanes in a double row. Dirk turned to Patch. "Anderson won't make it. I'll run out and ask him and come right back."

"Go to your marks!" the voice of authority boomed. The starter was standing at the line with the gun.

Patch turned to step into his lane, and Dirk grabbed his shoulder. "Wait till you've reached the end of the third lap," he said quickly. "See how you feel. Then do what you think best." He reached out to swat Patch, but Patch was already settling into his starting position.

"Get set!"

Two seconds later the starter's gun cracked, and Benny took off like a scared rabbit. Patch and Grover in the second row disappeared in a jostling mass of elbows and knees.

Mr. Anderson and Dirk leaned forward to watch the milers come down the stretch as they neared the end of the third lap. Fisher was leading Rawlings by fifteen yards. Ten yards behind Rawlings came Benny with Patch just behind. Three yards behind Patch was Cathedral's number-one miler. All five runners were using the

126

inside lane. Moving along in the second lane was Grover, just off the shoulder of the boy from Cathedral.

"Grover's stepped up his tempo," Dirk said. "He's taking that guy."

"He'll soon take Patch and Benny too, if he holds that pace," Mr. Anderson said. "He's picking up inches with every stride." The coach lowered his eyes to the stop watch. Benny was approaching the starting line.

Just as Benny crossed the midstripe and started the last lap, Mr. Anderson called out his time. "Three-thirty-three on the dot!" Benny heard him and smiled. At that same moment Grover moved up alongside Patch.

"Now!" Dirk said tensely. "Now we'll find out what Patch has decided. This is the lap where he stays or he goes."

Even while Dirk was talking, Patch seemed to swerve an inch or two to his right. But the road to the right was blocked by Grover. Patch cut back into line behind Benny; there was no place else to go. Grover's swift progress had halted, and now he was running shoulder to shoulder with Patch.

They saw Patch turn his head and say something to Grover, but Grover stayed where he was.

"Why doesn't Grover move up or drop back?" Dirk fumed. "Why won't he let Patch pass?" He had no sooner asked the question than the answer came to him like a kick in the stomach. "A box!" he wailed. "Grover's got Patch in a box!"

The coach was glowering down the track. "Patch invited it," Anderson grumbled. "He should've kept to the right, off Benny's shoulder—like I told 'im."

127

Patch slowed momentarily, hoping to drop back and run around, but Grover dropped back alongside him.

"It's too late now." The coach shook his head. "He can't break the record. Might as well stay where he is for a while."

Patch seemed to reach the same conclusion. The threesome moved onto the curve and around it, gliding along smoothly like planes in formation. Off the curve and onto the backstretch they moved, the formation unchanged.

"Grover can't hold that pace much longer—or can he?" asked Dirk.

"Neither can Benny." Mr. Anderson's eyes were narrowed as he watched the runners across the field on the backstretch. "We're losing ground."

"Naw . . . Fisher's just twenty yards ahead of Patch now, and he *was* twenty-five."

"Fisher made his bid in the third lap, as Benny predicted. Look at Rawlings. He's running a steady race, holding the pace we figured on."

Dirk watched the long brown legs rising and falling in perfect rhythm as the yards rolled away beneath them. "Yeah, he's fifteen yards ahead of Benny now and stretching the gap every second. How come? He's not going any faster, and Benny hasn't slowed down."

"Sorry to say, he has. Maybe Patch doesn't realize it either because Benny's knees are still pumping at the same rate, but his steps are shorter, a sign of fatigue. He's losing ground fast."

In the third lane the Cathedral runner edged closer to the trio, pulled abreast, and glided on past.

The three West milers were approaching the middle of

the backstretch, and Benny was motioning for Patch to pass. Patch veered to the right but nosed back in when Grover refused to yield. . . . Patch slowed down to run around, and Grover slowed with him. . . . Patch tried to dart forward and angle through, but Grover moved up and closed the gap.

At the midmark 220 yards from the finish, where his stint of pacing was to end, Benny glanced back over his shoulder. He seemed to jerk with surprise as he took in the situation. Dirk saw him say something in anger to Grover. And still the three moved along together.

Rawlings was a full twenty yards ahead of them now, and the tiring Fisher was plodding along still ten yards ahead of Rawlings.

"Something's got to give!" Dirk muttered. "Maybe Grover—"

Grover's head was beginning to flop from side to side with fatigue.

"Won't give out soon enough," Anderson snapped. "It might be too late already. Probably is."

Across the field Benny glanced back over his inside shoulder. He called something quickly to Patch and jumped off the track. Patch lunged ahead and left Grover floundering in his wake.

The lad from Cathedral was almost onto the curve when Patch overtook him. Patch leaned into the curve and drove himself around it as if he were running the 220. Emerging onto the straightaway, he was still far behind Fisher and Rawlings, who were chest to chest on the homestretch.

Dirk leaned over to look down the track. Back near the

129

curve was Patch, no grin on his face as he came pounding along toward the tape. The crowd was shouting deafeningly, but Patch didn't seem to hear. He swung out into the third lane, intent only on closing the gap. Fifteen yards from the tape he passed the faltering Fisher. But Rawlings' thin legs never varied a beat in their swift tattoo as he sped toward the finish.

"It'll take a fresh burst of speed to beat him," Anderson muttered.

"Patch hasn't got one left," Dirk said.

Three yards from the tape, Patch was a yard behind. He flung himself forward, snapped the tape, and would have fallen, had willing arms not rushed from the side lines to lend support.

Chapter 16

It was early evening. The city meet was over for another year. The last spectator had filed out of the East High stadium, and now a yellow school bus was nosing away from the curb. It was carrying a load of athletes westward across town, athletes still in their sweat suits, weary but jubilant.

"I've never broad jumped that far before, even in practice," Tom Martin was saying. He sounded amazed. "I felt like I was floating."

"You never know how you're gonna feel till you get out there on the track," Bill Adams replied. "I got away good, and I hadn't gone thirty yards before I knew that today I had it. I just felt right. It was my day."

"I don't know yet how I caught that hurdle," Mike Montgomery lamented. "Boy, that ground sure comes up fast."

Back in a corner Grover and Sax were talking in low voices. "How come you skipped up to the radio booth after the mile?" Sax asked.

"It's like this," Grover answered smoothly. "I'll be going to college next fall—here at Crescent City College.

131

I've always had a yen to be a radio announcer, and I've had some experience now on the school programs. So I asked the sports announcer to keep me in mind any time he needs someone to fill in."

"You talked to Harry Jenkins?"

Grover nodded.

"Grover Godwin, sports announcer. Ahhh . . . with that satiny voice you'd make a good disc jockey. Or better yet, you should advertise cosmetics."

"What kind of crack is that?"

"No crack a-tall. I can just hear you saying, 'Smoo-oo-ooth.' " Sax stared out of the window a moment and turned back to Grover. "They taught us in selling class always to wear a jacket and tie when we apply for a job. How comes a clotheshorse like you couldn't wait till he had his clothes on?"

Grover smiled. "Psychology, my pet. Timing and psychology. Those two things can work miracles."

"Such as," Sax prodded softly, "the miracle of a scarf dance on a race track?"

Grover shrugged. "Wouldn't you like to know?" He smiled sardonically. "Well, I'll say this. I've always maintained that running the mile is largely a matter of strategy. . . . You won't prove much, quoting *that.*"

Up toward the front of the bus, Moose was talking quietly too. "Boxing his own teammate!" he muttered. "Grover will never talk himself out of this one."

"You wait and see," Bill Adams answered. "Grover could talk himself out of a strait jacket speaking pig-Latin."

"Nah. This time he's overreached. He hasn't a leg left to stand on."

"Grover sprouts legs like a centipede."

The bus drew alongside the West High stadium and stopped, and the athletes swarmed out and into the locker room.

"Into the showers now, all of you," Mr. Anderson called. "All except Grover. Grover, you come into my office."

The two disappeared into the coach's office. The door, Dirk noted, was left standing open as always. And although the rest of the boys went about their business, the showers were strangely quiet.

"Your fine green satin ribbon," the coach began, "your ribbon for coming in fifth in the mile. Hang it on the wall above your bed. Look at it night and morning. Look at it before you say your prayers. Look at it before you put on your clothes to start a new day. Look at it now! *That's* what you sold your soul for! . . . It's the last ribbon you'll ever win at West."

Grover's voice was strong and cool. "That ribbon?" he asked and laughed. "No, Coach, what I did wasn't done for a ribbon—nor for myself. It was done to serve West High—and you."

"So how did you serve us today?"

"Today I gave you a second in the 880—*and a first in the mile!* The fifth is—inconsequential."

"Even the devil deserves his due. You gave us a second in the 880. But you tried with every muscle and every braincell to rob Patch of a first in the mile."

"Mr. Anderson, I think you'll find that you're wrong. I regard Patch as—as a willful young brother. Being older and wiser and more experienced, I've tried to look out for him, tried—you might say—to protect him."

Out in the locker room Dirk heard a disrespectful noise —like the muted blat of a nighthawk. Quick shushing noises cut it off, and silence resumed in the locker room.

"Just how did you try to protect him today?" the coach rumbled.

"I tried to protect him from himself. I boxed Patch— deliberately. Boxing, I know, is illegal. In doing it, I risked getting myself thrown out of the race. I risked an enormous blot on a record that's always been clean."

Grover was quiet a moment. Then he cleared his throat and continued. "I have great respect for Patch's speed. I also believe in—well, call it the innate dignity of man. I tried to prevent Patch from making a jackass out of himself—and out of his coach, his teammates, and his school —again, this time in front of all those thousands of people."

The coach grunted. "Go on."

"You remember last week," Grover said. "Patch ran a sensible race for three laps. In the fourth lap he cut loose and made monkeys out of us all, especially out of himself. You remember the indoor meet upstate. It was during the last lap, after he'd gotten bored with running, that he decided to play to the grandstand. It was during the last lap that he started doing the duck-waddle."

Out in the locker room someone remembered and snickered, and was quickly shushed.

"It was too big a chance to take in front of all those

134

people. Especially since crowds seem to be the incentive. So I kept Patch bottled up. I did it without your permission, I know. I didn't think you'd let me risk my reputation to win us this race, even though I was willing to. I kept Patch bottled up as long as I safely could. I had to let him loose while there was still time for him to overtake the others."

"*You* let him loose?" Mr. Anderson roared. "Benny did! Benny had to get clear off the track. Benny had to disqualify himself so Patch could get out of your clutches."

Grover's voice was humble. "Benny knew Patch's speed better than I did. I overestimated Patch. I was going to hold him for another three yards, but if I had, he might only have tied for first."

"Three yards from the tape he was still behind," Anderson mumbled.

"Well, that's how it was, Coach. I want to give you my word of honor—now—positively—that I will never again box anyone. I'll put up my uniform as forfeit if ever I do."

"It's been a strange season, Grover," the coach said, sighing. "You have more than today to explain. Two weeks ago in the meet with Central and North you were told to set a certain pace. Instead, you ran like a madman. Now, *I* know that *you* know—"

"Yes, Mr. Anderson, I usually do know exactly how fast I'm going. I knew then. What's more, I knew I was running the mile and not the 880. I just said that about the 880, I'll admit, because I had to give some kind of explanation."

"Well? Let's have the right one."

"You see, I'd read an article—about how Gunder the

135

Wonder Hägg once set a new world record because Arne Anderson set a very fast pace for him. I was trying to do the same for Patch. I didn't tell you that afternoon because—well—I'd run myself out, trying. I couldn't finish. I didn't take second as you'd expected me to, and I didn't want to seem to be putting the blame on Patch. It wasn't really his fault. It was all my idea, and I hadn't even told him about it."

If Anderson answered, nobody heard.

Grover's smooth voice went on. "You see, I've always tried to help and protect Patch. I think he's a promising runner—just sort of irresponsible. There was that business about the shoes. If ever I'd wanted to do him dirt, that was my chance. Instead, I told you I'd seen his track shoes packed in his bag. . . ."

The sound of a radio shattered the stillness of the locker room.

"Shut that thing off!" someone hissed.

"But this is the sport news!"

"Well, turn it up louder then. Let's hear what he says about the meet."

"Good evening, sports fans," a cheery voice greeted them. "This is your sports announcer, Harry Jenkins, bringing you news from the world of sports. But first, a brief word from our sponsor."

Two dozen boys in various stages of disapparel emerged like ants from an anthill. One of them was carrying a tiny portable radio. Through the door of the coach's office came Mr. Anderson and Grover.

After a few hundred words about beer, the bright voice of Harry Jenkins returned.

"West High carried off top honors in the annual battle of the local thinlies at East High Field today. A huge crowd, finished with the day's work, swarmed through the turnstile to watch the speedbursts and soarings, the thrills and the heartbreaks."

"Git on with it," Moose grunted.

The glib tongue of Harry Jenkins continued. "At the end of the meet, when the nip of evening was in the air, three city records lay shattered. Moose Elliot of West heaved the twelve-pound shot three inches farther than a local lad ever had heaved it before. Jim Perkins of East pushed the pole-vault record another half-inch skyward. And Lincoln's lithe Lawson Larrimore sped over the low hurdles a tenth of a second faster than last year, breaking his own city record.

"West copped the crown by collecting all points that they were expected to and adding two firsts that the experts had figured would go elsewhere. Senior Tom Martin turned in his best leap of the season to take first in the broad jump. Junior Patch Jones turned it on in the stretch to emulate another great stretch runner, Needles, and capture first in the mile.

"Foxy Coach John Anderson master-minded the latter event with as neat a bit of strategy as ever we've seen. He kept his runaway kid, the erstwhile playboy, locked in a box. Jones couldn't have chased a scarf or battled a windmill if he'd tried. His teammates didn't unlock the box until the last possible moment. Then Jones took off like a jack-in-the-box. Or rather, a jack-out-of-the-box. And West won the meet by that margin.

"Elsewhere across the nation today . . ."

A hand reached out and snapped off the set. A click, and the locker room was plunged into silence.

Mr. Anderson stood with his hands in his pockets and stared at the floor. As the silence grew, he looked up and found all eyes upon him.

"Get on with your showers, boys," he said gruffly. "You too, Grover."

Mr. Anderson wandered back to his office. Dirk heard the desk chair creak in protest as the coach slumped into it. Out in the locker room the boys looked at each other in astonishment a moment, before they all started talking at once.

"Into the showers with you," Dirk told them. "You heard what the boss-man said. I need those uniforms."

A few minutes later he heard the coach calling him. Dirk stepped into the office, his arms full of soiled uniforms.

"As soon as Benny gets dressed, send him in."

Dirk nodded. "He usually gets dressed pretty fast." Dirk lingered near the doorway. "Just get one boy straightened out," he said sympathetically, "and something else comes along to send things into a tailspin."

"Who's straightened out? Patch?" The coach shook his head. "He's taken the first step and a big one. But wait till he's done it on his own. No pressure, just self-restraint and dogged persistence. Sometimes it isn't scaling the peaks, it's slogging through the endless swamp that separates the men from the boys."

"Yeah. . . . Well . . . the team's all mixed up. They don't know *what* to believe about Grover. They've started to argue among themselves. Seems they expected Grover to have an answer, a slick one. But now they've gone and swallowed it. Some of 'em have, some of 'em haven't. They all want to hear what *you* think. I better warn you—that radio announcer convinced quite a few that Grover was not only telling the truth but is also a master strategist. Even—" Dirk hesitated. "Even—smarter than you."

Mr. Anderson studied his hands, folded on his desk, and said nothing.

"Coach, I'm not trying to tell you what to do, but some of those guys—if you kick Grover off the team for this—they'll think it's because you're sore that he outsmarted you."

The coach looked up. "See if Benny's dressed yet."

Benny was still buttoning his shirt as he entered the office. "Yes, sir?"

Mr. Anderson wasted no time. "When did you first notice that Grover was boxing Patch?"

"About midway of the backstretch on the last lap. When Patch was supposed to pass me and didn't, I turned around. I'd heard footsteps behind me but assumed they were Patch's."

"What did you say to Grover?"

"Not much. I was saving my wind at that point. I said, 'Move over.' He knew what I meant."

"What did he say? I want his exact words."

"He said, 'You make me.'"

"Grover told me he boxed Patch deliberately and was set to release him three yards farther on."

"I—yes—I'm sorry, sir, but we couldn't help hearing the conversation."

"That doesn't surprise me. Grover pitched his voice to the last row of the balcony—making his plea to the team, I suspect—and I didn't hold back either."

"If you want to know what I thought, sir, I didn't for a minute believe him. I wouldn't have dropped out of the race if I'd thought he planned to quit boxing a second later."

"I want to tell you, Benny. You did a very fine thing. One of the finest I've ever seen on a track."

Benny's eyes glowed. "It wasn't really so fine, sir," he admitted. "It was the only way I could think of to break the box. If I'd cut over in front of Grover to let Patch pass, the officials might have disqualified me. It seemed better just to drop out of the race so I wouldn't block Patch any longer."

Coach Anderson stood impulsively and gripped Benny's hand. "It's boys like you who keep me whacking away at this thankless job."

"Some day," Benny said wistfully, "I'll give you *real* reason to be proud of me. I won't be just—a good loser. I'll be a good winner, which is infinitely more difficult. Milers go on for a long time. . . ."

Suddenly it all spilled over, and he was talking rapidly —like one starved for the chance to talk. His accent became more noticeable. "I don't expect to be a really fine runner for a long time yet. Gil Dodds himself couldn't even finish the first Millrose race he ever ran in. Nine years —nine *years* later—in those same Millrose Games, he set a new world indoor record for the mile.

"Distance runners don't reach their peak till their mid-twenties or after," he hurried on. "Gunder Hägg was twenty-six when he set a world record for the mile. Glenn Cunningham broke the American record for the mile when he was twenty-eight and ran some of his best races after he was thirty. Gaston Reiff of Belgium was thirty-one when he set the world two-mile record.

"Too many Americans quit running when they leave college. No American has won the Olympic 'metric mile' since 1908—half a century! In fact, with one exception, no American has won *any* Olympic event longer than 800 meters, which is equivalent to the half-mile, since 1908! This country is crying for good distance runners."

"How right you are, Benny. Stay with it, and more power to you. You're aiming for the Olympics?"

"But of course."

"Then remember dashman Dave Sime, heralded as 'the fastest human'—till he pulled a leg muscle in the '56 Olympic tryouts and couldn't qualify for the American team. Remember what Roger Bannister said after the '52 Olympics. He lost at Helsinki, you know, and he realized then what a large part luck plays in sport. He realized that he'd staked too much on a single goal. . . . Running is not a life, Benny."

"I hope to do other things too, important things in biochemical research," Benny answered. "But one goal does not preclude the other. It's the ancient Greek ideal: a sound mind in a sound body. Plato, the Greek philosopher, was also a great athlete."

Mr. Anderson nodded. "Fit running into your life, but don't build your life around it. And do it for pleasure. I

141

sometimes wonder, Benny, if you get as much joy out of running as you might."

Benny glanced away and smiled. "After our first local meet I went to pick up my modest ribbon, and people I didn't even know spoke to me graciously. They congratulated me. I thought, this is very much worth the few hours of practice each week that it has cost me. Now—I find pleasure in practice too. I rarely think of my stride any more—and sometimes not even of pace. I feel the warm spring air rushing past my head. I feel the rhythm of my legs pounding out yardage with little effort. I know a new kind of pride. I feel the oneness and strength and smoothness. . . ." He stopped, embarrassed. "Aw—you called me in to talk about other things."

"Maybe so," Mr. Anderson said, smiling. "But this has done me more good. Just one further question about today's meet. How does Patch feel about Grover?"

"Patch? He hasn't told me. After your conversation with Grover and after the radio broadcast, Patch went into a shower. He hadn't come out yet when I left. . . . He—uh—took a water pistol in with him. Said he thought he'd figured a way to enjoy a shower."

Chapter 17

Dirk and Moose stood before the shining glass door of the radio station Monday noon as if they were rooted to the sidewalk.

"I dunno," Dirk mumbled. "Maybe this wasn't such a brilliant idea after all."

"Sure it was," Moose reassured him. "Only we gotta do it. We can't just stand here wasting our lunch period, wishing we'd already done it."

"But I don't know quite how to word the question."

"You know what you want to find out. Isn't that enough?"

"No. Any way I ask it, it's going to sound—well—nosy."

"Look, I don't mind missing my lunch—this once. But not just to stand out here on the sidewalk and yak."

Dirk pushed open the glass door with a sigh. "Sometimes I wish I'd never thought of this," he grumbled as he walked in.

They found themselves in a small foyer, sleekly modern, its walls adorned with one large clock and many slick photos of radio and TV performers. Dirk crossed to a desk on the opposite side.

The receptionist looked up. "Yes?"

"We'd like to see Mr. Jenkins, please."

"Harry Jenkins, the sports announcer," Moose said, coming up.

The receptionist shook her head. "I'm sorry. He's out of town."

"Out of town?" Moose wailed. "For how long?"

"Till next Monday. He's on vacation."

They looked at each other blankly. "Now what?" Moose grunted.

Dirk shrugged. "We go back to school. Hungry."

"Would you like to talk to Phil Patterson?" the receptionist asked brightly. "He's filling in for Harry this week. It just so happens he's in now."

While Dirk was hesitating, Moose answered, "We might as well."

"You go down this hall," she said, pointing, "and then jog left. His office is third on the right. I'll give him a buzz and tell him you're coming." She swung around to the switchboard.

As they walked down the hall, Dirk kept mumbling, "What'll we ask him?"

"Oh, well, at least we'll see what he looks like."

"Who cares?"

They passed a large room, its door standing open and its walls completely lined with shelves of records. A man in shirt sleeves was bending over, snatching a disc from the shelves here and there. "See you later," he said, addressing an invisible someone across the room. "I'm on in three minutes."

Dirk and Moose jogged left, past a drinking fountain

144

and under a large sign labeled QUIET. Several people scurried by in the silent hall. At the third door the boys stopped and knocked.

"Come!"

Dirk pushed the door open, and they stood in a cubicle scarcely large enough to be called an office. A chunky young man jumped up from a desk and beamed. "How can I help you, boys?"

Dirk cleared his throat. "We really came here to see Mr. Jenkins," he began lamely, "but they tell us he's on vacation."

"That's right. Anything *I* can do?"

"Funny time to take a vacation," Moose murmured. "End of April."

Mr. Patterson smiled. "Not really so funny. Not for a sports announcer. Basketball season ended last month, and baseball's just beginning to get up a head of steam. Before it's over we'll be into football. . . ."

"Sure, sure, it's all right," Moose said quickly. "We just —we wanted to ask him a question."

"Maybe I could answer it?"

"It's like this," Dirk said, taking over. "We wondered where sports announcers get their information—on local track meets."

"What kind of information?"

"The kind Harry Jenkins uses on his nightly sports roundup."

"Of course, but past or future?"

"Past. Like Saturday's meet."

"The city meet? Harry was there. In fact, he broadcast it. Only local meet all season that goes on the air."

145

"Well, I don't really mean what *happened*—like who won the events. I mean his opinions—for instance, on strategy. Who does he talk to? Who tells him the things he reports?"

Mr. Patterson shook his head. "I'm afraid you'd have to ask Harry that one."

"Yeah. Well. . . ." Dirk's voice was heavy with disappointment. "Thanks anyhow. I'm sorry to have bothered you."

"No bother at all."

Dirk moved toward the door, but Moose lingered. "What's this thing?" he asked, pointing to a long list that was propped on the desk near a small microphone.

Dirk glanced at it and read

Iharos	EE-hah-rosh
Rozsavolgyi ...	Ros-a-VOLE-yee
Sime	SIM
Tabori	TOB-or-ee

"Oh, that's Harry's," Mr. Patterson said. "We have to know how to pronounce the names of those athletes. He could look them up each time in some of these books—" He pointed to several reference books standing on the desk. "But when you're racing that sweep-second hand around the clock, and that little warning bulb up there above it has already turned red, you're not going to stop for something like that."

Moose nodded. "Uh-huh."

"Funny thing," Mr. Patterson remarked, "you're the second West High boy who has asked me that within the last hour."

"Oh?" Dirk said. "Who was the other one?"

The sports announcer lifted his shoulders. "I wouldn't know. He had on a jacket like yours." He indicated Dirk's senior jacket.

"Tall?" Moose asked. "Wavy blond hair?"

"Nope. Short and dark."

"Sax?" Dirk murmured under his breath. They shuffled around near the door, both wanting to ask what Sax —if it was he—had inquired about, but neither was quite that brazen.

"He—uh—came to see you today?" Dirk asked, groping to keep the subject open.

"About an hour ago," Mr. Patterson answered, nodding. "Well, no, not to see *me*. He really came to see Harry Jenkins." He leaned over his desk and began to glance at some papers. "Anything else, boys?"

"Guess not, but thanks a lot, Mr. Patterson."

They stepped out and closed the door. In the hall they stood for a moment just looking at each other.

"I'll bet it *was* Sax," Moose said.

"Could've been anybody—any senior—but I've got a hunch it was Sax."

"Cooking up something, you think?"

"I'd sure like to know!"

The bell clanged noisily as they entered the school building. From the way the doors started bursting open, spilling students into the hall, Dirk knew with relief that the bell marked the end of his lunch period and not the beginning of the period to follow.

Moose grabbed Dirk's elbow. "Sax has lunch the pe-

147

riod before we do. He had a class somewhere up that way this period. I know because I usually pass him in the hall. We've got four minutes to get to our classes. You want to come with me looking for Sax?"

Dirk started walking. "I'm with you."

Halfway along the hall they saw a flat-topped, square-jawed, sturdy figure approaching. Sax was wearing his senior jacket and red corduroys. Moose moved over into his path and stopped, forming a solid barrier.

"Hiya, Sax. Was your visit to the radio station successful?"

Sax froze. "What's it to you?"

"We've just come from the station ourselves," Moose said amiably. "We heard that you'd been there."

"What were *you* two doing there?" He sounded more curious than suspicious.

"We went in to talk to this Harry Jenkins guy."

Sax stared at Moose and turned to look inquiringly at Dirk. Dirk nodded confirmation. Slowly a smile spread across Sax's swarthy face. "I guess—maybe you two went for the same reason I did."

"Could be," Moose murmured. "What reason was that?"

Sax seemed to withdraw a little. "You oughta know," he rasped.

"I guess we do," Dirk said with an easy assurance he did not feel.

Sax laughed shortly. "We sure got nowhere, didn't we? The guy's off on vacation. Fellow who's taking his place, he's bubbling over with helpfulness—and no help at all."

"Well—Jenkins'll be back Monday."

Sax scowled. "Monday," he said significantly, "may be too late."

"Why?" Moose asked. "Why will Monday be too late?"

Sax glanced at his watch. "As the six-year-olds on our block say, 'See you later, Alligator!' "

Moose knew the answer. "After while, Crocodile."

Chapter 18

With a flourish Sax Warner circled the numeral 30 at the end of the page and flung down his pencil. "Mine!" he announced to the empty journalism office. It was sixth period Monday, one period before the deadline.

The door swung open, and Grover strolled in. "Enter the brain that pushes your pencil," Grover said airily.

"Too late. The poor thing wobbled along on its own and managed to turn out a column."

"I'll check it." Grover reached out and picked up the two scrawled pages lying on the table. "This it?" He started to read in silence but stopped and raised his head. "Where is everybody?"

"The National Honor Society got off two periods early today to go see something or other. Reward for doing something, I think."

"Explicit. That's what I like."

"Yeah, well, most of the staff are members. That's why they're gone. And how did *you* get down here?"

"Buster, I'm the Harry Houdini of the study halls. Chain me and lock me in a trunk—a moment later I'm free. Nothing can hold the Great Godwin."

"I see. You did it all with your tongue."

"Well, let's see if you did as well with your pencil." He glanced over the copy. "Hmm. Nothing special about the mile except that Patch won it. . . ."

Sax waited tensely, his eyes on Grover's face.

"You could," Grover began, "have said . . ."

"Listen, Great Godwin, I'm getting almightily tired of being your unpaid press agent."

Grover lifted his eyebrows. "Unpaid? . . ." He hesitated. "On second thought, *your* approach is probably better. So Patch won for a change. Play it down. Good idea." Grover waved his hand. "Leave it as is."

Sax sighed softly with relief and said nothing.

Grover read on. "You get pretty gaudy here, don't you, boy?" He read aloud:

> With the city meet successfully behind them, West thinlies now move along to the second of three big jamborees. Saturday will find the cindermen in Petersburg's sprawling stadium. A total of 586 athletes from 22 schools will vie in this, the 29th Annual Southern Indiana Invitational Track Meet, affectionately known as the Petersburg Relays. Crescent City schools are expected to dominate the huge affair, with West holding a slim edge by virtue of its triumph in the city meet.

Grover let the page flutter to the table.

"What's wrong with that?" Sax asked.

"Not a thing. Limpid prose. You were clairvoyant when you used the word 'affectionately.' You'll always remember the Petersburg Relays with special affection."

"How so?"

"Don't rush me. There's the little matter of the column to finish first."

"It's finished."

"News," said Grover, "is made every minute. An alert newspaperman like you should comment even on something that happened just before press-time."

"What happened?"

"Anderson happened. He called me out of study hall just now."

"And—?"

"As Anderson says, 'Gah!' . . . You've written a good column, Sax, but it's got to explain—favorably, of course —why Grover Godwin will run in the half-mile at Petersburg but not in the mile."

"He kicked you off the mile and kept you on the half! . . . How did he explain that?"

"He said I won't need to put myself out any longer protecting Patch."

Sax smirked but straightened his face quickly. "Did he say anything else that might indicate what he really thinks? Did he say, for instance, that you could try to redeem yourself in the 880? . . . No? . . . Did he tell you he'd spent the week end wrestling with his soul?"

Grover snorted. "That man has no soul. But you can wrestle with yours the rest of the period, telling your readers that Grover Godwin voluntarily withdrew from the mile to concentrate on the 880."

Sax shook his head. "Who'd swallow that? Better you don't—I don't—aw, whose column *is* this? Better we don't mention it. Not many students will make the trip to Petersburg. Most of 'em won't even know you didn't run both."

"Sax," Grover said beaming, "sometimes you show real promise. That's why I'm going to deal you in on a ribbon at Petersburg."

"Thanks, I'm doing all right on my own this year. I got a fourth in the city, remember."

"Petersburg's tougher," Grover warned. "Lots tougher."

"Not in the half-mile it won't be. Not this year. That Cannelton boy who beat everybody in sight graduated last June. I figure we'll finish about like we did last Friday. Sampson, Godwin, Englert, Warner."

Grover placed his fingertips together and studied them carefully. "How would you like to take second?"

"Or fly across the moon backwards?" He stopped and considered. "Sampson's bound to take first again. If I finish second, where would *you* be?"

"Now listen." Grover leaned forward and outlined his plan. "As simple as that," he said when he had finished. He smiled and spread his hands.

"Nope. No thanks." Sax leaned back shaking his head. "Not me. Not *this* little chickadee."

Grover waited, still smiling. He drummed on the table with his fingertips. "Well?"

"Not me," Sax repeated. "Include me out."

"I think," Grover said softly, "you'll want to reconsider."

"Why should I?"

"Maybe—to stay on the team?"

Sax sat very still for a moment. Then he leaned forward, chin jutting. "I've got news for you, Grover. You've reached the end of the line with that threat."

"How so?"

"I can match you now. *You* talk, *I* talk."

"Oh?"

"I drove downtown during my lunch period today," Sax began. "Went to the radio station."

Grover waited, his eyes narrowed.

"I called on your old friend Harry Jenkins," Sax went on.

"Good," Grover said casually. "Of course, he's not really my old friend. First time I ever laid eyes on the man was Friday, and that's the truth. Well, anyhow—what'd old Harry know?"

Sax wavered a moment. "Harry knew—all kinds of interesting things."

Grover looked at his fingernails and smiled. "Such as?"

"Such as—how he came by certain information last Friday!"

"Oh? . . . That sounds promising. Tell me more." Grover was plainly enjoying himself, and Sax was beginning to squirm. "Information on what?" Grover prompted.

"On the mile," Sax said, his voice tight.

"Good. I wondered where he got the idea that old Griz Anderson had planned that stroke of genius. What'd he say?"

"He said—you told him so."

"*I* told him?" Grover asked, looking astonished. "Oh, no. All I did was ask him about substituting next fall. I told you about that Friday night. . . . You sure you didn't misunderstand him, Sax?"

"Positive!"

"In that case," Grover said, rising, "I'd better phone him right now and tell him he's way off base." Grover walked over and laid his hand on the phone. He waited.

Sax flushed and squirmed and started to protest, then reconsidered. "Go ahead and call him," he mumbled.

Grover dialed three digits and stopped, hand poised, to glance at Sax. Sax was gripping the edge of the table with both hands, staring straight ahead. He turned when the sound of dialing stopped, but said nothing.

Grover dialed two more digits, and the school bell clanged, ending the period.

Sax leaped up and started for the door. He turned back and snatched up his column. "Gotta turn this in to Mr. Perkins," he muttered. "Right away!"

He dashed through the door and slammed it behind him.

Grover cradled the receiver gently. He looked at the door and smiled. "Sax," he murmured in the empty office, "you should've listened to Harry's Sunday-night broadcast. He said he was leaving at midnight last night for a week of deep-sea fishing off the Florida Keys."

Grover strolled to the door. "Maybe I'll try deep-sea fishing myself some day. But why bother? I can catch fish on dry land."

Chapter 19

In the Petersburg dressing room Saturday afternoon Dirk Ingersoll was kneeling at the feet of Bill Adams, swabbing Bill's knee with alcohol. "Does it sting?" Dirk asked.

"Kinda. It's just a scrape though. Lucky I fell after I'd passed the finish line. Be okay for the relays."

"Sure," Dirk said, putting a gauze patch over the abrasion. He glanced at his watch and turned to Benny and Patch, who were sitting at the other end of the bench. "They'll be calling the mile in five minutes. You two ready?"

Patch had removed one shoe and was smoothing his sock. "Ready, willin', and able," he sang out. "Well—abler. Abler than ever before." He patted the stop watch that lay on the bench beside him.

Benny took a swig of honey, screwed the lid on the plastic bottle, and tossed it to Dirk, who slipped it into his pocket. "Patch, it's amazing," Benny said, "the progress you've made this week in learning pace."

"Credit Dirk with an assist," Patch answered.

"It was your idea, Patch," Dirk put in. "All I did was show you the quarter-mile landmarks along the road. *You're* the little man who's been running home every night, timing each quarter."

Patch grinned. "If I hadn't been thick in the head, I'd have started a lot sooner." He pulled on his track shoe and tied the lace firmly, double-knotting it. "It didn't dawn on me till the city meet what the coach was talking about long ago when he said, 'First know yourself and then your opponents.'"

"What made it penetrate finally?" Bill asked.

"The city meet. I had a chance to break the city record. Dirk asked me, 'Can you do the last lap in such-and-such?' . . ." Patch shook his head. "Me—jolly little Jonesy—I didn't have the foggiest notion what I could do. Well, sir, I decided right then to find out as soon as possible."

"How fast can you run the mile?" Bill asked.

"In 4:32." Patch smiled and stood up. "And pace myself too," he added, proud as a small boy.

"At last. Say, what's the record for the Petersburg Relays?"

"It's 4:32.5," Benny said quickly, rising also. "Set by Tommy Deckard of Bloomington in 1934—before we were born. Oldest record on the books here."

"Why, Patch, maybe you—"

Patch and Benny were moving toward the door, their spikes clattering on the concrete floor. Each had a hand on the other's shoulder.

"Good luck, both of you," Bill and Dirk called after

them and rose to follow. Benny was already out of the
door and singing very softly.

Ich hat' einen Kameraden,
Einen bessern findst du nicht . . .

"Benny seems different today," Bill commented to
Dirk.

"Yeah, relaxed. The pressure's off. No pace to set for
Patch. No Grover to look out for."

They moved out into the bright sunshine. It was warm
for the end of April, the sky dazzlingly blue, the air almost balmy. On the field and along the side lines
swarmed a small army of athletes.

The loud-speaker boomed. "First call for the mile
run!"

At the end of the third lap Patch was floating along far
in the lead. Body erect, head high, shoulders relaxed,
he was covering ground with deceptively easy-looking
strides. Now and again he glanced at the stop watch he
held in his hand.

"Maybe he'll do it this time!" Dirk gloated. "Sure wish
I knew his time, but Rawlings and Fisher are no slouches,
and look where they are—almost fifty yards behind
Patch."

"And look who's right on their heels!" It was Benny,
in fourth place, shuffling along with his economical heel-
to-toe roll. Didn't know he could keep up with those
boys," Bill said.

"He can't. Or—he couldn't . . ."

While they were talking, Patch had moved onto the

curve. At the far end, just before he came off onto the backstretch, he turned and looked back over his inside shoulder.

"Benny!" he shouted, seeing his teammate still in contention. Patch waved one arm to motion Benny onward, then regained his stride and continued along the backstretch.

"Look at Anderson," Dirk muttered a little later, "standing there near the finish line watching his stop watch as if his life depended on it."

"Time must be good. Anderson's really excited."

Patch was rounding the last curve. As he approached the homestretch, he turned and looked back again over his inside shoulder. A grin swept his face and he shouted, "C'mon, Ben!" Benny was still fourth, five yards behind Fisher, who was trailing the smooth-striding Rawlings. Rawlings, in second, was now sixty yards behind Patch. Patch waved to Benny again.

Coach Anderson's face turned red. He leaned out over the track and shook his fist. Patch, just coming onto the homestretch, looked up, glanced hastily down at his stop watch, and lost his smile. His spikes started biting into the cinders more rapidly.

"Anderson's gonna squeeze that watch dead," Bill muttered.

Patch flashed down the track to the finish line, snapped the tape, and trailed off. Anderson, back at the finish, jerked out a handkerchief and mopped his brow, then turned his attention to Benny.

Rawlings' machine-like gait was carrying him toward the finish a certain second. Fisher was still third, but

Benny was accelerating quickly and evenly. Ten yards from the finish he passed the fading Fisher and crossed the line in third place, his head thrown back and his weary face wreathed in a smile.

"How'd he ever do it?" Bill murmured.

Dirk shook his head in disbelief. "If I were Benny, I'd tell you, 'There is a precedent.' I saw it happen—saw it on TV. Remember when Landy came to this country in '56 to run a four-minute mile?"

Bill nodded.

"Nobody had ever broken that barrier in the United States," Dirk went on, "and everybody turned out to see him do it. Fellow named Bailey, another Australian but not in Landy's class as a runner, was part of the field. After all, *some*body had to run against Landy. So Bailey, whistly and joyful 'cause all *he* had to do was run, catches up with the great Landy near the head of the homestretch. Bailey gives Landy a swat on the rear and steams past him—and goes on to win by a stride. Wins it in less than four minutes!"

"Yeah, I remember something about that. Never quite understood it though. Bailey had never even come close to four minutes before."

"Guess it just goes to show, when a coach tells you, 'Run relaxed,' he isn't just making noises."

The loud-speaker boomed again. "Results of the mile run. . . . First, Jones of West. . . . Time . . ." The announcer's impersonal voice became edged with excitement. ". . . 4:32.1, setting a new mile record for the Petersburg Relays!"

An hour later Dirk and Coach Anderson were staring unhappily at the score sheet on Dirk's clipboard.

"That's the sad story, Coach. We've got to win both the 880 and the last relay to win the meet. We'd figured on Grover coming in second in the 880, but that was when we were counting on Moose to get first in the shot-put. How come Moose only got third? I was inside fixing Bill's knee and missed it."

Mr. Anderson sighed. "His third heave was far and away the best of the day. Moose knew it too, the minute the shot left his hand. He got so excited he started leaping around in the circle."

"Yeah?"

"So he faulted with his left foot. The heave didn't count."

"Oh . . . well, that leaves it up to Grover—or Sax."

"Neither one can come close to Sampson," the coach said, shaking his head. "But at least they can try. I'd better tell them just how we stand so they'll know how much depends on their trying."

"And quick," Dirk said. "The starter is already walking over this way."

Coach Anderson motioned Grover and Sax out of the mob of half-milers and explained briefly. They listened intently and even, Dirk thought, smiled a little.

When the coach had finished, Grover gave Sax a long look and said, "Mr. Anderson, we'll try our best to come through for you!" He hesitated. "I think we can do it."

At the end of the first 440 Grover was still holding the lead he had grabbed at the start. Five yards behind

161

Grover came Sampson, running well within himself, conserving his strength. Three yards behind Sampson and off his shoulder was Sax.

"You think Grover can hold the lead, Coach?" Dirk asked anxiously.

"Frankly, no. I think it'll be a repetition of last week. Sampson's a chaser. He likes to have somebody else set the pace for the first lap and a half. Then in the last 220 he cuts loose and wins in a driving finish. When Sampson uncorks his sprint, Grover can't hope to match it."

"Guess you're right," Dirk conceded in disappointment. "Somehow I'd hoped that Grover might do something—like setting a faster pace."

"This is his usual pace, but it's also his best, his top speed. All he can hope to do is maintain it."

The runners were on the backstretch now and nearing its midmark, the last 220, when Sax Warner suddenly spurted. With a burst of speed he charged up alongside Sampson and let out a yell of delight. It wafted across the field and sounded like "Hey!"

Up ahead, just at that moment, Grover limped on one foot and seemed to go lame.

"What's happened to Grover?" Dirk wailed.

Grover hobbled a few steps and then, just as quickly, recovered and resumed his stride. He began to run smoothly again, still in the lead.

"Whew!" Dirk gasped. "Had me worried for a moment."

Coach Anderson was watching in tense silence. The runners had passed the middle of the backstretch and were moving along in tight formation, Grover directly ahead of Sampson on the pole and Sax alongside Sampson on his right.

"Say!" Dirk muttered. "It's past time for Sampson to make his bid. Why doesn't he start it?"

"How can he?"

Dirk looked again and felt himself go hollow inside. "Grover and Sax have him boxed," he murmured, aghast.

The boxed Sampson seemed slow to accept the fact that Sax would not be leaving his side, either driving forward or dropping back, in a moment or two. The trio was on the curve before he began his struggles to free himself, and there it was hard to judge what was going on. Near the end of the curve Sax glanced back to check on the runners behind. One man had moved up to within five yards of the threesome.

As Grover, Sampson, and Sax pounded onto the homestretch still in formation, Mr. Anderson glanced at his stop watch. "They've slowed down a little. Grover's setting the pace a shade under his best time—so Sax can keep up," he muttered.

"Maybe Grover hurt his foot," Dirk said weakly. "Maybe Sax doesn't realize that he's boxing Sampson." Dirk leaned over for a better view down the stretch. "Look at Sax, Coach. Look at his face. Look at his neck muscles stand out. He's giving it all he's got. He couldn't pass Sampson now if he had to! And you can't blame him for trying to keep up!"

Thirty yards ahead of the runners the tape was

stretched taut across the track. Sax risked another glance over his shoulder. Out in the third lane the runner in fourth place had edged to within two yards of him.

The crowd was on its feet, screaming. Dirk saw Sax open his mouth. He seemed to shout something, but Dirk couldn't hear it.

Ten yards from the tape Grover was still ahead by a stride. Behind him, shoulder to shoulder across the three inside lanes, were Sampson, Sax, and the interloper in one horizontal line. Sax was beginning to falter. A moment later he was flopping like a rag doll and losing ground fast. The horizontal line buckled, forming a shallow V.

Into the opening flashed Sampson, into the lane which Sax had just vacated. Sampson started to swing around Grover. But Grover was already snapping the tape.

"We did it!" Dirk shouted. "We did it! That's one leg of the trophy. Now for the final relay, and maybe we'll carry it home—that great big beautiful trophy."

Coach Anderson stood and glowered. "I've got to be sure," he muttered, "I've *got* to be sure. . . ."

Ten minutes later the announcer called out the results of the shuttle-hurdle relay, the final event. After the cheers had risen and died, the somber voice continued. "And now, for the presentation of the trophy, we switch to the field and Superintendent Mansfield of Petersburg."

Down on the field was bedlam. The West boys were leaping and prancing, patting one another, and shouting with joy. Well-wishers were darting in and out of the group. In the midst of the clamor stood Mr. Anderson, eyes closed and brows knitted in fierce concentration.

"Friends . . ." the clear voice of Superintendent Mansfield rang out.

Anderson's eyes snapped open. He grasped one boy by the arms and moved him aside and pushed his way through the team. He strode to the microphone, where Mr. Mansfield stood holding a huge trophy topped by the gold figure of a runner. The coach drew Mr. Mansfield aside and started to talk rapid-fire.

The superintendent's smile vanished. He asked a question and shook his head. He asked another and nodded toward the microphone. Together the two men moved to the microphone. Still holding the trophy, Mr. Mansfield leaned forward and began again.

"Friends," he said, and his voice sounded strained, "the coach of the West High team, John Anderson, has just been telling me—something. I've asked him to say it to all of you."

He stepped aside. Mr. Anderson moved over and grasped the microphone shaft in both hands. His knuckles showed white.

"I believe," the coach began slowly, "that a victory won dishonestly is worse than defeat—infinitely worse. There is no disgrace in losing. The disgrace lies in winning dishonestly. Therefore . . ." He paused. ". . . I have just asked Mr. Mansfield to award the trophy to the runner-up school."

A gasp went up from the stands and cries of dismay from the team.

"The judges were generous," Mr. Anderson continued. "I refer to the 880. You saw it. There must have been doubt in the minds of the judges. If so, they did the right thing in not calling a foul. They leaned over backward to be fair. There has been no complaint from the other team, probably for the same reason. Now the time has come for us to match these people in sportsmanship."

He cleared his throat and drew a deep breath. "I believe that the boxing you saw in the 880 was an intentional foul, committed for the purpose of preventing the best runner from winning the race. I believe it strongly enough that I hereby forfeit our victory in the 880." He paused. "Our margin of victory for the meet was only one point, including points won in the 880. Therefore, we lose."

He stepped back while the crowd sat in stunned silence. Immediately he stepped forward again and inclined his head toward the microphone.

"To the other boys on our team I want to say this. You who earned points in the other events still have your own victories, all of which you gained fairly. These personal triumphs are yours to keep. My decision takes nothing away from your efforts. We simply were not the best team today. Now we go home with our hands empty but clean. We know that an old and honorable trophy is still bright. In the trophy case at West it would only have been a tarnished testimonial to our vanity, a daily and taunting reminder that the price of victory *can* be too high."

He stepped back. Slowly a ripple of applause came drifting across the track from the grandstand. It burst

166

into thunderous sound. In a moment every spectator in the stands was on his feet clapping and shouting.

The West High boys lifted their faces, chagrined and angry, bewildered and proud.

And the sound of applause swept across them.

Chapter 20

The boys had stood by in silence and watched Mr. Mansfield award the trophy to their jubilant opponents. Now Mr. Anderson turned to his team. "We'll go to the bus," he said. "Straight to the bus, where we can talk in private."

They hurried out of the stadium and clambered aboard the bus. Mr. Anderson said a few words to the driver, who left, and the coach closed the door behind him.

"Now," said Anderson, standing at the head of the aisle. "We'll talk this thing out if you like. If anyone wants to express an opinion, this is his chance."

There was pin-drop silence for a few seconds. Then from a seat near the front came Grover's voice, coolly indignant. "Will somebody please explain to me what this is all about? . . . I ran a clean race. I led all the way. I never once weaved out of my lane. I broke the tape—no question about it. Then *you* get up and make a speech about the disgrace of the 880. Somebody comes and takes my blue ribbon out of my hand. If something went on behind me, I wouldn't know. I never looked

168

back. But I don't see yet how anything else could change the fact that I won—and won fairly."

The low rumble of voices was indication enough that others shared Grover's opinion.

The coach turned to Sax, who was sitting beside Grover. "How about it, Sax?"

Sax squirmed in his seat. He leaned forward and gripped his knees with his fingers. "I caught up with Sampson on the backstretch. I thought I could pass him. I tried, but I never could make it. I wanted to finish second, and I hung up there just as long as I possibly could."

Again the low rumble of teammates' voices.

Mr. Anderson jingled a couple of coins in his pocket and looked out the window. In a moment he turned back to Sax. "In that case, how did it happen," he mused, "that when Sampson dropped back on the curve, you dropped back too?"

"I was—momentarily winded."

"*Each* time Sampson dropped back to run around behind you, you got momentarily winded?"

"Yes. He had the pole, and on the curve I had farther to go in the second lane."

"But each time that Sampson darted forward to shoot through the gap, you shot forward too. How could you do it, being winded?"

"I guess the strength just came to me. I knew how bad we needed the points. You'd told us before the race, and we promised to try."

"The moment to pass your opponent was when he was dropping back. Every runner knows that."

169

"Yessir."

"Yessir, what?"

"I knew it too, but that's when I didn't have it. The strength."

"It sort of came off and on like a flashing light?"

Sax did not answer.

"Grover," the coach snapped, turning suddenly, "why have you been writing Sax's column?"

"I guess your boy Friday Ingersoll told you that," Grover sneered. "Yes, sometimes I suggested an improvement in Sax's column. Why? Anything wrong with that?"

"Sax, did you ask for Grover's help or merely accept it?"

"I—accepted it."

"Why?"

Sax shrugged.

"Why did you reluctantly accept Grover's help, Sax?"

"Grover can be pretty clever sometimes."

"You mean—when he suggests to his girl friend that she let her scarf blow down the track ahead of Patch?"

The team gasped in surprise. To them the girl was still Madame X, a total stranger who had vanished wraith-like into the crowd.

"Is that what you mean by cleverness, Sax?" the coach prodded.

"I don't know anything about the scarf."

"But you do know about today. It was clever of Grover, wasn't it, to remember Sampson's pattern for running a race? It was clever of Grover to suggest that you come up alongside Sampson just before he started his drive. It was clever of Grover to ask you to give him

170

a signal so he'd know when to drop back and close up the box without turning his head. That part was especially clever. It gave him a chance to say that he'd run a clean race and never looked back. But it sure left you holding the bag!"

Sax did not answer.

"So you followed instructions and yelled, 'Hey!' And Grover promptly pretended to turn an ankle or pull a muscle so he would seem to drop back for a reason—though not the real one. Did Grover tell you he planned to do that?"

Sax sat in silence.

"But strangely, when he heard Sampson a few feet behind him, he made a complete and miraculous recovery. That wasn't so clever. . . . And then he got clever again. He kept running his clean race, not turning his head, while you had to battle it out with Sampson to keep him boxed. That was *really* clever of Grover—because it nailed *you* with full blame. If someone had been disqualified, it wouldn't have been Grover."

Sax sat in sullen silence.

"He gave you another assignment too. He knew he was running a little slower—so you could keep up—and he made you the lookout to warn him when someone got close. He couldn't afford to look back. . . . What place did he promise you, Sax?"

Sax shook his head.

"So someone got close, there near the finish, and Grover's boy *Warner* lived up to his name. You shouted a warning. And Grover stepped up the pace. He went off and left you behind. Grover wanted that blue ribbon bad, and the devil could take the hindmost. The hind-

171

most was you. . . . What place did he promise you, Sax?"

Sax did not move.

The coach jerked around. "How about it, Grover?"

Grover chuckled. "This Grover guy seems to be quite a schemer. Clever—but dastardly. It'll disappoint you to hear that he really isn't. He's just a hard-working runner. . . . All I know is that I ran a clean race with my eyes straight ahead."

"Sometimes limping and sometimes not. Eyes straight ahead, depending on Sax to keep you informed. And he did. He did all that you asked. Everything!"

"What Sax did is none of my business." Grover shrugged with indifference. "Whatever he did, he did on his own. Maybe he boxed the guy, maybe he didn't. *I* wouldn't know. *I* was in the poorest position of all to see what he did."

Sax's rasping voice was suddenly clear in the hushed bus. " 'I can talk myself out of anything.' . . . That's what you told me, Grover, and that's what you meant. No more and no less. Talk *yourself* out of anything, and the devil can take the hindmost. That's me."

"What place did he promise you, Sax?" the coach asked softly.

"Second . . . but I only got fourth."

Mr. Anderson did not comment, and for half a minute nobody spoke. Then Sax's voice came again, wheedling. "You told us before the race we needed a first to win the trophy."

"So I did," Mr. Anderson said. "But after I told you, you and Grover didn't have time to talk—not even a second. No, I can't buy that, Sax. This scheme was hashed

172

up in advance, planned to the smallest detail before you ever left Crescent City."

Sax looked down at his feet. "Last Monday," he admitted, nodding. "I guess I don't belong on the team," he mumbled. "I guess I should turn in my suit. . . ." He lifted his head and laughed shortly. "And the funny thing is, I only did it to stay on the team. I had to do what he told me—or else."

"Or else what?"

"Ask Grover."

Grover raised his eyebrows. "I don't even know what he's talking about."

Sax turned to Grover. "I'm talking about—shoes!"

"Shoes?" Grover asked blankly.

"The shoes," Sax said, turning again to the coach, "that disappeared out of Patch's duffel bag before the first meet—the indoor meet. I took 'em. I don't know why. It just seemed smart at the time. I figured I couldn't lose. I wouldn't be going upstate, and no one would think I'd done it. Patch wouldn't run his best in shoes that were too big. And maybe he'd look like a harebrain and get the heave-ho. Or maybe you'd figure that Grover had done it, and Grover would get the sack. Either way, I stood to gain. But none of it happened." He sighed. "I didn't steal the shoes though. I just put 'em back in Patch's locker." He stopped, and a look of surprise crossed his face. "I can tell you this now," he said, almost as if explaining the fact to himself. "I only did it so maybe I'd get to run the mile and double my chances to earn a letter. But now I know that I'll never own one. . . ."

"Did Grover see you taking the shoes?"

"He said he did. But now I'm beginning to wonder. He was sitting outside in his car when I left the stadium. It was after practice and late. Everyone else had gone home, but Grover was sitting there talking to some babe. I'll swear they come up out of the ground like ants when Grover's around. . . . He didn't say anything at the time, but the Monday after the indoor meet he told me he'd seen me do it. Said he saw me opening Patch's locker."

"Did you see him, Grover?" the coach asked.

"Of course not," Grover snapped. "If I'd known anything about it, I'd have told Dirk when he asked me—up at the State Relays. You'll recall that I stood up for Patch and told Dirk I'd seen Patch putting the shoes in his bag."

"That," said Sax, "was so he could prove that somebody took them out—and name me—whenever he chose. . . . I don't know yet if he really saw me. But he pulled a good bluff, and he knew that I knew the combination to Patch's locker."

"How did you know it?"

"That was my locker last year."

Dirk clapped a hand to his forehead.

"So that," Sax went on wearily, "was why you kept reading in my column about the Great Godwin. It was always—do it or else. I tried to get something on *him*. I even went down to the radio station and tried to see Harry Jenkins. I wanted to ask him what Grover had told him."

"What do you mean—what Grover had told him?" the coach demanded. "When?"

"Last week—at the city meet—when he boxed Patch in the mile. Soon as the race was over, Grover streaked up to the radio booth. I asked him why. He said—to apply for a job."

The team burst into raucous laughter, giving vent to pent-up emotions. They sobered and stared belligerently at Grover.

Grover was flushing. "You didn't have to sell the team short today, Mr. Anderson," he said. "You didn't have to give their trophy away. *They'd* won it, not *you.* My nose was clean. Nobody could ever have proved or even suspected a single thing. Not of *me,* and I'm the guy who took first and got us the points that won us the trophy."

"Don't think I didn't consider that, Grover. And don't think a trophy like that means nothing to me. But I just don't do business that way. Sure, any trophy that we can win fairly belongs to the team. But these boys are basically decent, Grover. If we'd had time to thrash the thing out and put it to a vote, they'd all have rejected that trophy. We didn't have time, so I did it for them."

"I ran a clean race," Grover repeated. "I never looked back, I never cut over—"

"Grover," the coach interrupted, "I remember something you told me last week. 'Coach,' you told me, 'I want to give you my word of honor—now—positively— that I will never again box anyone. I'll put up my uniform as forfeit if ever I do.' "

Anderson jingled the coins in his pocket and glanced out the window.

"Try to talk yourself out of that one, Grover," he said in a quiet voice.

175

Chapter 21

When the bell rang on Monday morning, Miss Murdock pushed back her chair and picked up the sheet of paper that a scurrying messenger had just deposited on her desk.

"Attention, homeroom!" she called in her best drill-sergeant manner. "Now hear this—the morning bulletin." With as much fervor as she could muster she read aloud, for the thousandth time in her teaching career, the announcements of the day.

> The seniors will meet in the auditorium during homeroom period this morning to select commencement invitations.

At the mention of commencement every face in the room looked brighter—perhaps reflecting her own, she mused. She read on.

> Book Club members, remember the picnic at Burton Park after school this afternoon. Please be prompt.

She sighed. You can't get to June without living through

May and school picnics, she thought grimly. She hurried on to the next item.

Congratulations to Mr. Anderson and the track team for taking second place in the Petersburg Relays Saturday. Sherrill Jones broke the twenty-three-year-old Petersburg Relay record for the mile.

"Who's Sherrill Jones?" a voice piped.

"Right in front of you," Miss Murdock sang out. "Stand up, Patch, and take a bow."

Patch shoved back his chair and stood grinning foolishly. After a round of applause he asked, "Can I sit down now?"

"You may." She laid the sheet on her desk. "Patch, you ran a fine race Saturday. You led all the way. I assume that that means you set your own pace?"

Patch beamed. "Yes'm."

"You mean you were there, Miss Murdock?" somebody asked.

"Even schoolteachers go out of town once in a while," she snapped.

"To a *track* meet?"

"I happen to live near Petersburg," Miss Murdock explained. "I was home this week end and drove in to Petersburg Saturday because—well—two of my boys are on the team, Patch and Moose. Moose did all right for himself too, though he's done better—and will again next Saturday in the Ohio Valley meet."

"You think she really knows about pace?" a boy whispered.

Another boy shook his head and sniffed, "Probably thinks a track is something a train runs on."

"Or maybe," Miss Murdock said, bristling, "that a pole vault is a mausoleum constructed of poles." She turned again to Patch. "Listen, Patch," she said, "Benny Chapnik's a fine boy, but why don't you wave to him somewhere else?"

"Huh?"

"Twice Saturday," she said, "you looked back and waved Benny on. Do you know what happened to John Landy in the Mile of the Century at Vancouver when he looked back from the same spot, just before the end of the last bend?"

Patch shook his head.

"That's where Roger Bannister passed him. And there was Landy, still looking back over his other shoulder—unsuspecting, unprotected, losing valuable time when he might have been responding to Bannister's challenge. Bannister himself said that that was one of the main reasons he was able to beat Landy."

"It's okay, Miss Murdock," Patch said soothingly. "Nobody passed me."

"Patch Jones," she demanded, "do you think you can look around and wave and face forward again without losing time?" She put her hands on her hips. "Patch, say 'a thousand and one.'"

Patch said it.

"That," she announced, "took you one full second. What would your time have been Saturday if you'd frittered away one more second?"

Patch figured. "Woulda been 4:33.1."

"So," she said, spreading her hands, "no record. So—don't look back!"

"Yes'm," Patch answered, grinning. "Don't look back. Might trip."

"What I want to know," somebody blurted, "is why that wool-headed coach gave back our trophy!"

"Yeah, how 'bout that?"

"I read—" someone began.

"Who does Anderson think he is?"

Miss Murdock started to speak but stopped when Patch rose with a quiet dignity she scarcely knew he possessed.

Patch looked around at the outraged faces. "Mr. Anderson was right," he said firmly. "We didn't have time to vote on it—the team, that is—but after we heard the facts, you can take it from me, we knew he was right."

From across the room Moose rumbled, "I know how you kids feel. I felt like—like I was opening my mouth to take a big bite of cake when somebody snatched it away and threw it into the garbage."

"Yeah! Yeah!"

"But listen!" Moose hurried on. "When Mr. Anderson stood up there in front of all those people and looked at that great big trophy and said that we didn't win it fair, so we didn't really win it, so give it to the guys who deserve it—man, I'm tellin' you, I was proud. And when all those people yelled like their lungs would bust, I got goose flesh along my backbone. The way they yelled for our sportsmanship—that was better than any old trophy."

179

Miss Murdock waited a moment for that to sink in before she picked up the morning bulletin and finished reading it to her homeroom. She laid the sheet on her desk. "Any questions?"

"Yeah. Did Patch chase a scarf Saturday?"

Suddenly everyone joined in.

"I'd go to all the track meets," a girl said, "if Patch would always run after a scarf."

"What did he do that was funny?"

"Did he take off his shoes? Did he count right?"

"Us guys on the team," Moose interrupted, "we think a clown is fine—if he also produces. If he doesn't, he'll be like the midget who batted for the old St. Louis Browns or the outfielder who played in top hat and tails. He'll just—disappear."

"I still want to see him do something zany."

"He hasn't done anything funny for a long time," a girl complained.

A boy answered gruffly, "So he ain't so funny these days. He's winnin' now, ain't he? What d'ya want?"

"Barney," Miss Murdock said primly, "you took the words right out of my mouth."

Chapter 22

Up in the radio booth atop the New Albany grandstand, a sports announcer glanced at his watch, ground out his cigarette, and pulled his microphone toward him. He leaned over it cozily, glanced at his watch again, and started chatting.

"Good afternoon, sports fans, from the New Albany stadium. This is Lip Dominic bringing you the play-by-play—if you'd call it that—of the Ohio River Valley Invitational Track Meet. Seventeen of the finest prep track teams from up and down the Beautiful Ohio have been invited here to battle it out this afternoon. It's a beautiful day in New Albany—if you don't look up. There's a big black cloud scudding toward us along the river. Oh, well, as our teachers taught us, May showers bring April flowers.

"Out on the field," he continued, "athletes in a full assortment of sizes are warming up for the hundred-yard dash. Up here in the stands you can almost hear the excitement crackle. . . ." He stopped a moment and cocked his head. "Or is that thunder? . . ."

Half an hour later the sound was that of a beating rain. Down in the dressing room the nonparticipants were huddling about like bedraggled chicks.

"Maybe," Bill Adams muttered, "Grover and Sax are the lucky ones after all—sitting in a nice dry movie, I'll bet, back in Crescent City."

"Even with wet feet," Benny said, "nobody here would trade places."

"That's what I like about you, Benny," Dirk said. "You're so literal. . . . Hey, listen! The rain's slacking."

"That's not what I hear," Moose grumbled. "They're calling the shot-put." He walked to the door and looked out. "Patch, where's that old johnboat you use in high water?"

"Better try walking," Bill advised. "Not on the cinders but across the field. Maybe you'll pick up enough mud on your shoes that you won't feel like dancing."

"Don't worry," Moose answered grimly. "I'll never footfault again. Well, I guess I better get out there and start warming up." He started through the doorway.

"Give yourself a *real* talk today, boy," Dirk called after him. "Get some lightning and thunder into it. Stomp around in the mud till it squeaks. Then give that old shot a ride it'll never forget!"

They stepped to the door to wave at Moose's broad back.

"Rain's stopped," Patch said, "but the field looks like a hog wallow. Think they'll go on with the meet?"

"Sure. The storm didn't last long," Dirk said. "Look, they've already got fellows out there trying to sweep the water off the track. They'll be calling the mile soon."

182

"Better get into your lanes now, boys," Mr. Anderson said to Benny and Patch. "And good luck!"

"Up there," Patch murmured, pointing off to the southeast, "is a rainbow."

Mr. Anderson turned and smiled at it. "A sign that our troubles are over."

Dirk nodded. "A new month, a rainbow, and no more Grover and Sax. One of you two oughta win this."

As Patch stepped into his lane, the runner in the next lane turned and stared. A glimmer of recognition came into his eyes. "Hi, goof," the boy grunted.

Patch turned, saw a total stranger, and bowed to him ceremoniously from the waist.

"Aren't you the character," the boy asked, "who duck-waddled across the finish line at the State Relays?"

Patch nodded.

"Well, this is nice weather for ducks. You oughta finish better than last today."

"Know something?" Patch asked. "I intend to."

The starter moved into position and raised his gun. "On your marks . . ."

Up in the radio booth Lip Dominic's spirits were still undampened, his chatter unquenched. "The milers are leaning forward for a standing start," he rattled. "What a gang of them—must be a couple of dozen. That sound you hear is the crowd drawing in its breath. There's the white puff of the starter's gun. Hawlick, the red-headed, stork-legged Louisville ace, bursts ahead. But someone is flashing out from the seventh lane. He's grabbing the lead. It's—uh—Jones, Patch Jones, of Crescent City.

183

Hawlick has already disappeared in the swirl of colliding bodies. But we'll see him again! Just last Saturday Hawlick ran a 4:28 mile.

"These boys are starting off mighty fast with a long way to go. They're already at the first turn. There's the inevitable jam. . . . Now they're coming off the turn. Hawlick swings wide to pass, but that Jones boy isn't caught napping. He's sprinting too.

"Now they're floating along the backstretch, all of them. This is poetry in motion. The power, the grace, the integration. Smooooooth. Smooth and effortless. The human body trained to perfection. Give me the joy of watching men running, and you can have your jalopy races.

"The field is beginning to pull apart, dividing themselves into pacers—and racers—and chasers. . . . Here they come past the starting line at the end of the first lap. Jones is leading by ten yards. Hawlick is second. Thompson of Henderson, Kentucky, third. The rest of the runners are mud-spattered. Not just their legs. Their trunks and their jerseys. A few even have a dab of mud on their faces. The track is sloppy. Puddles of water standing along the outside lanes—but nobody's running out there.

"The leaders are on the curve again. Jones starts to look back. Changes his mind—for some reason. The crowd—usually silent at this point in the mile—is already talking it up. They know that they're seeing something special. A couple of mighty fast milers out there holding a mad, a frantic pace on a water-soaked track. It can be done. John Landy did it—ran the second fastest mile in history, a blistering 3:58.6, on a sodden track. . . .

"Here comes Jones past the grandstand again, starting the third lap. He's twenty yards out in front now, and Hawlick is still second. . . . We don't know much about Jones. A newcomer to the mile. But so was Don Bowden of California when he broke the national collegiate freshman mile record in 1955, the first time he ever competed in that event. . . . Patch Jones is a little guy. Wiry. Five-feet-eight and 135 pounds. But then, Paavo Nurmi was little too. So are those hurryin' Hungarians who keep smashing the distance records. . . . Jones won the Petersburg Relays last week, setting a new record, and they tell us he wasn't pushed. They tell us nobody knows how fast he could actually run, if pushed. . . .

"That pop you heard was the gun—to signal the start of the last lap. Jones has opened a thirty-yard lead. Nobody's keeping up with the Joneses today. But nobody! . . . Some of the trailing runners will soon be lapped, but what's a little more mud in the face?

"Jones is already on the backstretch, his powerful legs still churning—steadily, obediently, tirelessly—turning this into a one-man show. . . . He's rounding the last curve, coming onto the homestretch. He starts to look back, changes his mind again. He's on the stretch and opening up with a finishing sprint.

"Oh, what a finishing kick! Jones is drawing on all his power and all his speed as he charges headlong for the tape. Like the fullback who drives for the extra yard. Like the baseball great who can call forth that extra ounce of speed to beat out the throw to first. . . . Only. . . ." The announcer's voice became muffled with confusion. "Only—there's no one behind Jones. No one closer than half the length of a football field. . . ." His voice trailed away.

He was back a few seconds later, ebullient again. "Jones snapped the tape and staggered into the eager arms of supporters. Here come the others. Hawlick of Louisville, second . . . Murphy, Paducah, third . . . Brumbaugh, New Albany's number-one miler, fourth . . . Thompson of Henderson, fifth. . . . I'll see if I can get the time. . . ."

A moment later he announced in a voice that crackled, "Unofficial time for the mile—4:22.2! I'll have to check, but I think that's the fastest mile ever run by a high school student in Indiana. The state record is 4:22.3, set in 1951 by Lambert of Muncie.

"This is the decade of tumbled barriers—the sixty-foot shot-put, the seven-foot high jump, and of course the four-minute mile. Ever since the mile run leaped into headlines around the world, high school runners have been chopping away the seconds. In 1955 the national prep mark was lowered to 4:19.5. In May '56 a St. Louis boy clipped it to 4:19.2. Just two hours later a senior from De Kalb, Illinois—Jim Bowers—dropped it to 4:16.1. . . .

"Well, as Schmerz said—he's the man who dreamed up the internationally famous Millrose Games held at Madison Square Garden each year, and he's seen all the great ones. As Schmerz said, 'You never know where they'll come from, but if you look hard enough, you

186

might see them on their way.' . . . I think we've just seen a boy on his way."

Down on the field, slowly and painfully, Patch was beginning to recover his wind. "Who was it?" he gasped. "Who was it?" His eyes fell on Benny. "How'd you do, Ben?" he asked.

"Seventh."

"Oh—sorry."

"It's all right." Benny was puffing too. "I'd rather lose a fast race—than win a slow one. Long ago—I learned to wait. . . . Congratulations! You were superb."

"Gee, thanks." Patch turned to the coach. "Who was it?"

"Huh?"

"Who was it? Who was the guy that hung right on my heels all the way? I had to run faster'n I thought I *could* —to beat him."

Coach Anderson shook his head. "Nobody. After the first lap, nobody was even close. You were all alone out in front."

Patch looked bewildered. "Right behind me," he mumbled. "Spattering mud on my legs. All the way to the tape. I had to run like the devil. Couldn't let up. He stayed right on my heels, spattering mud—"

"Spattering mud on your legs!" Poker-faced Benny doubled over with laughter. "I did it too—spattered mud on the backs of my own legs. Same as you."

Two hours later the spectators, drenched and then sun-dried, had roared the last relay runner across the finish line. Now they were waiting patiently for the yard-high trophy to be presented. The sun was beaming its gayest, and Anderson likewise.

"Just our day," he told the reporter. "For once, every man turned in his top performance. All at the same time, a minor miracle. And on the right day, a major miracle."

"Sorry, I missed your first words," the reporter said, scribbling. "The noise of that siren—"

Anderson repeated. "I can't tell you how happy we are," he added, "to have won this handsome trophy. All the boys did their best. I'm proud of 'em!"

"Especially Jones?" the reporter asked.

"That boy's come a long way. What he did today he couldn't have done at the start of the season. It takes more than speed and stamina to make a great miler."

The reporter glanced at the team, sweat-suited, assembled, and awaiting the presentation with mounting impatience. "Which one is Jones?" he asked.

Coach Anderson looked his team over proudly. "He's— he's— Hey! Where's Patch?"

Bill Adams jerked his thumb toward the gate. "He went thataway."

"Did you hear the siren?" Dirk asked. "Patch covered his ears. He sat on the ground and grabbed his ankles. And still it kept howling. Patch jumped up and ran as if the guy with the pitchfork was after him. . . . Patch always chases fire engines, Mr. Anderson. And this one sounded so much bigger, he said, than the one they had in Millville."